MISSING IN MUDBUG

JANA DELEON

CHAPTER ONE

MARYSE ROBICHEAUX LEJEUNE stepped out of the shower, dried off, and pulled on her robe before stepping into the bedroom. Her husband, Luc, had left for work ten minutes before, a lingering look of worry on his face as he'd walked out the front door. Maryse knew whatever case he was assigned had him rattled more than usual, but all her attempts to broach the subject had been met with stonewalling on his end. The only thing she'd gleaned from him was a fear for her safety.

Keep all the doors and windows locked and when you leave the house, take your gun. When driving, make sure you check your rearview mirror to ensure no one is following you. Do not go into the swamp for any reason. If you have a world-ending emergency there, let me know and I will make plans to take you out myself.

Being a DEA agent, Luc was always cautious, but the past week, he'd really gone to a different place. And despite the fact that she tried not to dwell on whatever dangers Luc faced every day doing his job, Maryse was jittery and on edge. The hot shower had momentarily helped, then she'd stepped out of it to hear a repeat of Luc's admonitions before he left for work, and she'd launched right back into a case of nerves.

As she passed the bedroom doorway, she saw a shadow move in the living room. Instantly, she froze, her heart pounding in her chest. What if the bad guy Luc was worried about had been watching the house? What if he'd waited for Luc to drive away so that he could kill her or kidnap her or even worse? A couple seconds later, her cat, Jasper, scrambled into the bedroom and slid under the bed.

Maryse inched over to the nightstand and pulled out the loaded nine millimeter with suppressor that was always there. Gripping the gun tightly, she crept out of the bedroom and down the hallway, struggling to keep from hyperventilating. With every step, she said a silent prayer that all the training Luc had given her with the pistol paid off.

When she got to the edge of the hallway, she heard rustling on the other side of the wall. Before she could change her mind, she jumped around the corner, gun leveled.

The man in the black mask stood at the far end of the dining room near the kitchen counter. Maryse screamed and fired off five rounds in succession. Her aim was dead-on, but the bullets passed right through the man and struck the hutch behind him, glass exploding with every shot. A second later, the man started screaming, and Maryse knew it wasn't a man at all.

"Damn it, Helena!" Maryse yelled, not sure whether to stop shooting or go back to her bedroom for more ammo. "What are you doing in my house?"

"Why are you shooting at me?" Helena wailed. "You know I hate that."

"Because you look like a burglar. Why are you dressed all in black?"

"No one else can see me, so I figured why not?"

"*I* can see you and I thought you were here to kill me."

Helena waved a hand and the black mask vanished. She glanced back at the mangled hutch, then gave Maryse a sheepish look. "I guess I didn't think about you seeing the outfit and not knowing it was me. Sorry."

"Sorry? Sorry! You have two seconds to get out of my house or I start firing again."

"This was just a misunderstanding," Helena said.

"One. Two."

"Oh shit." Helena darted through the wall.

Maryse ran out the front door, waving the pistol, and chased her down the street all the way to the woods a good two blocks away.

Maryse skidded to a stop at the tree line and stared into the foliage, deliberating taking a parting shot at the ghost, but finally decided it would be a waste of a perfectly good round. Frustrated at the mess of glass she was about to have to address, not to mention the probable need to purchase a new hutch, she dropped her arm to her side and headed back up the street to her house.

She hadn't made it half a block when Sheriff Colt Bertrand walked out Big Freddie Pinchot's front door and stopped dead in his tracks, staring at her.

Crap. I'm wearing a robe and holding a gun. I'm going to get a psych hold.

And that's when Maryse decided that Colt might just be the most intelligent person in Mudbug. Without so much as the lift of an eyebrow, he dug his truck keys out of his pocket, jumped into his vehicle, and drove away without even a backward glance.

———

"You can't just walk up to someone's kitchen window and steal their pie." Jadyn St. James stood in Mildred's office at the Mudbug Hotel, hands on her hips and frowning down at Helena Henry, who was practically inhaling the cherry pie on the desk in front of her. The fact that the rather large ghost was decked out like a cat burglar in black spandex was even more troubling than the stolen pie.

Mildred, the hotel owner, stood next to her, shaking her head. "We had this discussion last year before you left. You're a ghost, Helena. You don't need to eat. You can't possibly."

Helena looked up at them, red cherry pie filling dripping down her chin. "But I want to eat. Do you realize that I can't get high cholesterol or diabetes, and I won't gain a pound from this? Now tell me you wouldn't do the same."

Jadyn looked over at the plump hotel owner and knew she'd just lost her ally. No matter how much Mildred hated Helena constantly stealing food from her hotel refrigerator, she wasn't about to let it make her a liar. Jadyn had little doubt that given the criteria Helena listed, Mildred would spend every day eating like Helena was right now.

For that matter, so would Jadyn.

She looked down at Helena and sighed. "Okay, I get it. At least, as much as anyone can. But you can't steal things in broad daylight from people who can't see you, although that's probably a blessing. But you're going to give someone a heart attack. Not to mention that you'll make it impossible for Colt to do his job when people start reporting the thefts, and then residents will give him holy hell for not arresting the bad guy."

Helena waved a hand in dismissal. "Sophie Jenkins is an old drunk. Everyone is just too polite to say it. So even if she reported a whole bakery marching out of her house, no one in Mudbug would believe her, least of all Colt."

"I hate to say this," Mildred said, "but she's right. Sophie's sorta known for her outlandish statements. A floating pie wouldn't so much as raise an eyebrow in this town."

Jadyn threw her arms in the air. "This town cannot be your personal buffet."

"If they had a decent buffet around here," Helena complained, "it wouldn't be a problem. Not like anyone would miss an egg roll or two or a handful of popcorn shrimp. I tried the high school, but it was horrible! It's no wonder half of the kids sneak out behind the school and smoke pot at lunch."

Jadyn closed her eyes. "I did *not* just hear you say that."

"I said—" Helena started.

"No," Jadyn said. "What I meant was, I'm going to pretend I didn't hear that part about the students, and that if you'd like to repeat it, you should do so in front of the sheriff."

"He can't hear me and besides, why should I be the one to tell?" Helena asked. "One of his deputies was out there last week smoking with them."

Jadyn looked over at Mildred, who didn't look any more pleased with that bit of information than she was.

"Okay, bottom line," Jadyn said. "You don't steal food from anyone who is not a drunk. And don't steal from anyone who can't afford the loss."

"Fine," Helena grumbled. "You two act like I'm an archcriminal."

Jadyn shook her head. "I can't believe I just endorsed stealing food, albeit under specific terms."

Mildred patted her on the back. "Knowing Helena tends to skew normalcy a bit."

Jadyn opened her mouth to reply but before she could get a word out, the front door to the hotel opened and slammed shut.

"Helena!" Maryse yelled from the lobby. "Don't think you're getting away with it."

Instantly, Helena dropped the piece of pie she'd been holding, jumped up from the chair, and ran through the wall behind her. A couple seconds later, Maryse stormed into Mildred's office, her face flushed red.

"Where is she?" Maryse demanded.

"She just ran through the wall," Jadyn replied, wondering what in the world Helena had done to get her normally even-keeled cousin so angry.

"I'm going to kill her." Maryse stared at the wall and yelled, "I'm going to kill you!"

For a split second, Jadyn wondered if it were possible to kill a ghost—which would solve a lot of problems—but then figured Maryse's rant was rhetorical and not literal. "Should I even ask?"

"Oh, you should ask all right. Then when I have Sabine exorcise her back to whatever pit of hell she crawled out of, you won't feel a bit of sympathy."

Mildred looked over at Jadyn and raised an eyebrow. "What happened?"

Maryse took a deep breath and then unloaded on Jadyn and Mildred, filling them in on her less-than-stellar morning.

"The hutch that I gave you as a wedding present?" Mildred asked.

Maryse nodded. "It's riddled with bullet holes now."

Mildred put her hands on her hips. "I may just have to kill her myself. That hutch was a family heirloom."

Jadyn cringed, quickly deciding silence was her best option.

"That's not even the worst part," Maryse said. "One of the vases on the hutch that I shot was daddy's urn."

Mildred paled and Jadyn's hand involuntarily flew up to cover her mouth.

"I must have grazed the top of it," Maryse continued, "because it fell onto the dining room rug and the top part broke off. Which would have been a situation that was salvageable except that while I was chasing Helena down the block, Jasper decided it was a perfect spot for a new litter box."

"Holy Mother of God!" Mildred made the sign of the cross.

Jadyn felt her stomach clench. Next time she saw Helena, she might be tempted to try shooting her, too.

Maryse flopped into an office chair. "I rolled up the whole

mess in the rug and tossed it in your Dumpster. I hope you don't mind."

Mildred sank into the chair next to her. "Your daddy is in my... oh, well." Mildred grabbed a magazine off the desk and started fanning herself. "I don't want you worrying about this. I'll give you half of my ashes, and we'll find you a sturdier urn."

"Do they make them bulletproof?" Maryse asked.

Jadyn's hand slid from her mouth and she looked back and forth between the two women, a million thoughts racing through her head. She assumed Jasper was a cat and he'd committed the worst of offenses with Maryse's dad's ashes and ruined a perfectly good rug. But why in the world did Mildred have some of Maryse's dad's ashes? Was it a Mudbug tradition? Some weird agreement among residents? And where was Mildred keeping her portion? Because she was going to be a lot more careful around vases now that she knew what might be contained in them.

In the midst of her mind storm, a flash of an old friend—an artist welder—went through her mind. "I might know someone who can handle the bulletproof urn thing. Let me check into it."

Maryse and Mildred both stared at her for several seconds and finally Maryse smiled. "You're serious, aren't you? You're really going to contact someone about making me a bulletproof urn?"

Jadyn froze, wondering if she'd misread the situation. "Yeah, I mean...that's what you want, right?"

Maryse nodded and sniffed. "I'm not good at girlie stuff, but that's so nice, I don't even know what to say."

Jadyn looked down at the floor and shuffled her feet. If Maryse was "not good" at girlie stuff, Jadyn was practically allergic to it. "Seems like the right thing is all. You helped me get the game warden position here, and you and Mildred have really made it easier to fit in."

"I brought you here and exposed you to Helena," Maryse said. "If I were you, I'd kick my butt."

Jadyn smiled. "Maybe after I've had more coffee."

Maryse rose from the chair and nodded. "I think breakfast sounds like a great idea. Shall we head over to the café?"

Jadyn's stomach rumbled and Maryse laughed.

"I guess that's my answer," Maryse said.

"Watching Helena eat must have made me hungry," Jadyn said. "Hey, would it be horrible if I had pie after my eggs?"

"I hope not," Mildred said, "because that's what I plan on doing. Let me put up the sign."

They followed Mildred to the front desk where she put the "Back in thirty minutes" sign on the front desk.

"I don't have anyone booked for today, so no check-ins," Mildred said and she switched the phone to voice mail. "If anyone shows up without a reservation, they can come back in thirty or sleep in their car."

"Perfectly reasonable," Jadyn agreed. "Let's get some breakfast."

They crossed the street to the café and Jadyn automatically gravitated to a vacant booth in the far corner. She'd quickly learned that Maryse and Mildred's topics of conversation were not always the "for public consumption" type, especially with talks of Helena thrown into the mix. Sitting in the back, away from the other patrons, allowed conversation with no leaning over the table and whispering. Leaning and whispering got in the way of eating. And right now, Jadyn was starving.

Maryse and Mildred nodded approvingly at her selection as they slid into the bench across from her. A pert waitress popped over a couple of seconds later to take their order and leave a decanter of coffee. Jadyn poured a round for everyone, took a big drink, and decided she may as well get answers to the questions roaming through her mind.

"I have to ask," Jadyn started, looking directly at Mildred, "and if you don't want to answer, just tell me it's none of my business, but why do you have some of Maryse's dad's ashes?"

"Maryse's mother died when she was four, and afterward her daddy was understandably a mess," Mildred explained. "But a child doesn't stop growing or needing things while their parent gets their life together, so I stepped in and did my best to give Maryse a maternal connection."

"You were wonderful," Maryse said. "Still are."

Mildred blushed a bit. "Taking care of Maryse meant I was around an awful lot and after he stopped grieving so hard, well…"

"You started a relationship," Jadyn finished. So much about Maryse and Mildred's relationship now made perfect sense. She'd known the women were close but hadn't realized that Mildred had essentially stepped in to raise Maryse right after her mother's death.

Mildred nodded. "We started as friends at first and stayed that way for a good long time. I wasn't anxious to jump into anything. I got no problem being a self-supportive woman. And Maryse's daddy loved her mother more than anything. It took a long time for him to decide he wasn't being disrespectful to her if he cared for me."

"But you never married?" Jadyn asked.

"No, and that was fine too. We were both older and stuck in our ways to the point that living separately was better for us than living together. I honestly don't think we would have lasted if we'd been under one roof."

Maryse nodded. "I loved him to death, but Daddy was the most difficult man on the face of the earth. Mildred and my mother should both be up for sainthood."

The waitress stepped up to the table and slid plates in front of them. Jadyn seasoned her eggs and dug in as soon as everyone had a plate. For several seconds, the only sounds coming from the table were of satisfied customers.

"You know," Jadyn said, "Mudbug may just have the best food I've ever eaten."

Mildred nodded. "I definitely think the catfish are the best here than anywhere else, but there's a woman in Sinful, a bayou town a little over an hour from here, who makes banana pudding that is so fantastic there are actually city ordinances about it."

"No lie?" Jadyn tried to imagine what sort of laws could be cultivated around dessert.

"No lie," Mildred said. "I was visiting a friend one weekend and managed to get a bowl. It was downright heavenly. I tried to coax the recipe out of the café owner, but she said she's taking it to the grave."

The bells over the top of the café door jangled and they all looked over to see Colt stroll inside. As he walked toward the counter, he looked their direction and smiled. Jadyn immediately felt heat rush up her face, but as he turned around and she looked across the table at Maryse, she realized the grin may not have been for her benefit. Her cousin looked simply mortified.

"What's up with you and Colt?" Jadyn asked.

Maryse gave them a guilty look. "I may not have told you guys everything that happened this morning."

"Why the heck not?" Mildred asked.

"Because the rest was embarrassing," Maryse said.

"Well now you have to tell us," Jadyn said.

Maryse sighed and told them about running down the street in her robe, waving a gun.

"Of course," Maryse continued, "I'm not even thinking about any of that until I see Colt walk out of Big Freddie Pinchot's house."

Mildred shook her head. "Big Freddie must be making those UFO sighting calls again. He really should lay off the bottle."

Jadyn had to laugh. "I wish I'd seen that. What did he do?"

"He stopped short and stared for a couple of seconds," Maryse said, "then he just hopped in his truck and drove away, cool as a cucumber."

Mildred gave an approving nod. "Smart, if you ask me."

"I thought the same thing," Maryse said.

Jadyn grinned at her cousin, the visual of a gun-toting, robe-wearing Maryse so vivid that she almost felt like she'd seen it herself. "That may be one of the funniest things I've ever heard."

Mildred laughed. "Yeah, but if it's all the same, I hope the good sheriff doesn't look the other way every time a resident is strolling around in a robe and waving a handgun."

Jadyn stared. "Is that really a problem?"

"Happens more than you'd think," Maryse answered.

Jadyn shook her head. Mudbug had to be one of the strangest places she'd ever been. She wasn't sure what it said about her that it was also the first place she'd felt like she belonged. "Maybe I should buy a new bathrobe...just in case."

Jadyn knew she shouldn't have looked, but she couldn't keep herself from glancing over at the counter. At that exact moment, Colt turned around and their eyes locked. He gave her a wave with his free hand and headed out of the café.

Maryse glanced at Colt as he left and then narrowed her eyes at Jadyn. "I thought you were going to have a run at the sheriff, but so far, you've disappointed me."

"Is that part of the job description?" Jadyn asked "Because if hooking up with the first single man I meet is a requirement, I need to ask for more money."

Maryse looked over at Mildred and they both grinned.

"Told you," Maryse said.

Mildred shook her head. "You didn't tell me nothing I hadn't already seen. Like you're some big romantic. Luc practically threw himself across her to get her attention. Man had to save her life to get a date."

Maryse rolled her eyes. "Whatever. Anyway, technically Colt

has already saved Jadyn's life, or she saved his, or both. That's all beside the point. The fact of the matter is, they've faced death together so now they should take things to the next level."

Jadyn smiled. "Jumping into bed with someone comes after a near-death experience? Seems a little rushed since I ran into trouble my first day on the job."

"So you're an early bloomer," Maryse said. "Anyway, you've already learned how life can be taken away in an instant, so I think you need to get on with things."

Jadyn picked up her fork and stabbed at her apple pie. She knew her cousin was half joking with her, at least about the requirement for sex after almost dying, but the truth was, Jadyn had done a lot of reflecting after everything that went down in the graveyard with Colt. For every ounce of flamboyance that her mother had, Jadyn had matched it with a conservative one. To the point that for a couple of years now, she'd been almost going through the motions rather than existing in the moment.

It was something, she decided, that needed to change, but not by hopping into bed with Colt Bertrand. Although she had to admit, there were worse ways to step outside the box. Still, a relationship wasn't something Jadyn was ready to navigate. She was already working through a new job, a new town, and new friends and family. A man—even a man as hot as Colt—would only complicate things. They always did.

She was wondering whether to formulate a reply or change the subject when she noticed something moving at the end of the table. Before she could manage anything but pointing, the hand that extended from the wall grabbed Mildred's pie and pulled it clean through the wall.

"Damn it!" Marysc popped up from the table and everyone in the café stopped eating and stared.

"It's not stealing if I know you." Helena's voice sounded from the outside wall. "It's borrowing."

Maryse clenched her fists and for a minute, Jadyn thought she was going to open one of the back windows and vault out after Helena, but Mildred leaned over and grabbed her arm.

"Sit down," Mildred hissed.

Maryse looked back at the gawking patrons. "Sorry, folks. I just realized I forgot my vitamins."

She sank back into the booth and glared at the wall. "She's getting worse."

Jadyn shook her head. "How can taking Mildred's pie be 'borrowing' when she has no ability to pay you back?"

"Oh, she could pay me back," Mildred said. "She could pay us *all* back by taking a long vacation in another state. But the likelihood of Helena going anywhere that she doesn't have a captive audience is slim to none."

"How can she do that, anyway?" Jadyn asked. "I mean, Helena's not real, per se, but the apple pie was. So how did she pull it through the wall?"

"We don't really know," Maryse said. "It's not like Helena came with a manual. She's figuring out new things all the time. The problem is, they're never consistent."

Mildred nodded. "At the Johnson wedding, she tried to make out of the reception hall with an entire tray of hors d'oeuvres. She made it through the wall just fine, but the tray smacked right into it and dropped to the floor."

"Made a helluva mess," Maryse added, "and got a couple of men who saw the whole thing banned from the open bar the rest of the night."

"I wish I couldn't see her at all," Jadyn said. "It's already a fine balance, knowing what she does and trying to look the other way, but making up plausible explanations for the things she does is likely to get us all branded as crazy."

"Or arrested for running down the street waving a gun and wearing a bathrobe," Mildred said.

"There is that," Maryse agreed. "Let me flag down the waitress and get you another slice of pie."

"Don't bother," Mildred said. "I need to get back to the hotel anyway. I'll grab a slice to go at the counter on my way out."

"I need to get going too," Jadyn said. "I'm trying to map ten new miles of bayou each day until I feel like I know where everything is."

"Don't get too comfortable," Maryse said as she rose from the booth. "One hurricane and it could all change. That's why the set of maps you have now is worthless."

Crap. Jadyn hadn't even thought about the hurricane factor. The weather variances between north and south Louisiana made her job so different.

As Maryse tossed some bills on the table, her cell phone rang. She pulled it out of her pocket and frowned.

"It's Luc," she said.

Mildred climbed out of the booth and watched Maryse closely, a worried look on her face. Jadyn got the impression that a midmorning call from Maryse's husband was anything but normal.

"What happened?" Maryse asked, her voice rushed and an octave higher than usual. "What about Raissa?"

Jadyn glanced over at Mildred, but as soon as Maryse had mentioned Raissa's name, she'd frozen in place, not even blinking.

Agonizing seconds crept by and the blood drained from Maryse's face before she disconnected the call. "Luc's at the hospital. Zach was rushed in an hour ago."

Mildred sucked in a breath. "What about Raissa?"

Maryse shook her head. "He wouldn't say. He just said to get down to the hospital." Maryse pulled her keys from her pocket and dropped them on the floor. She stared at Mildred, her eyes stark with fear. "What if Raissa is dead?"

"We don't know that," Mildred said. She reached over to pick up the keys and dropped them herself. "Damn it!"

Jadyn grabbed the keys. "I'll drive."

"You have to work," Maryse protested.

"It will wait." She pulled some money from her jeans pocket and left it on the table, then ushered the two women out of the café. Jadyn didn't know much about Raissa and Zach except that they were good friends of Maryse's and Mildred's. But if Luc insisted on a face-to-face, the situation couldn't possibly be good.

As they climbed into Maryse's truck, Jadyn said a quick prayer that whatever had happened, Maryse's friends wouldn't be hanging out with Helena anytime soon.

CHAPTER TWO

Luc was standing in the emergency room lobby talking to Colt when they walked in. Jadyn felt her heart beat a little stronger when she saw the sheriff. *It must be bad if Colt is here*, she thought, trying to convince herself that her reaction to the man was because of the situation.

Maryse immediately ran over to Luc and he pulled his wife into a quick hug. Jadyn lagged back, uncomfortable being present in the midst of a private situation.

"Don't just stand there," Mildred whispered, "get over there and find out what's going on."

Jadyn shook her head. "Raissa isn't my friend. I would be intruding."

"But Maryse and I are your friends, and I'm afraid we might need someone to lean on later."

Mildred grabbed Jadyn's arm, giving her no choice but to walk over to where the others stood. As she and Mildred approached, she gave Colt a nod before looking at Luc, waiting for the news.

"I was working a job this morning," Luc said, "and we came across Zach on the side of Old Mill Highway. He was unconscious and it looks like he was hit by a car."

"His car was hit?" Maryse asked.

"No. We haven't located his car yet. It appears as if he was struck while on foot."

"And Raissa?"

Luc shook his head. "We found no sign of her, but the search-and-rescue dogs are on their way."

"Maybe she wasn't with him," Maryse said. "Oh God! She probably doesn't know what happened."

"According to their handler at the FBI," Luc said, "Raissa and Zach were on their way back to Mudbug last night. They left New Orleans around nine o'clock after wrapping up the case they'd been working the last couple of months."

Jadyn's pulse quickened. No one had ever told her that the couple worked for the FBI. And if they had a handler, that meant they worked undercover. That explained the heightened concern she'd felt as soon as she entered the hospital.

"You think the handler's telling you the whole story?" Colt asked.

Luc shook his head. "I don't know. He sounded as confused as we are, but even if he knows anything, he's not about to tell me."

Although it was frustrating, Jadyn understood the bureau's policy. If Raissa and Zach were still on a case, it was likely that everything about and leading up to this incident would be confidential. "Any sign of their car?"

"Not yet."

"No GPS?"

"No," Luc said. "They were in Raissa's personal vehicle."

Colt frowned. "Was there any sign of a struggle?"

"It was impossible to tell if any hand-to-hand combat took place, but we found Zach's pistol several feet away from him. The magazine was empty."

"How many rounds?" Colt asked.

"Seventeen. We found all the casings on the highway."

Jadyn's heart dropped as Luc's expression went from worried to grim. She knew he was running through all the possibilities that flooded her own mind, and like her, he hadn't found a single one that was favorable for Raissa.

"Look," Colt said, "this is all outside of my jurisdiction, and I assume the FBI will take lead anyway, but I'll get in touch with them and see if I can get in the middle of it somehow."

Luc nodded. "I appreciate it. They're certainly not going to let DEA know anything."

A doctor walked through the emergency room doors and over to Luc. "You brought in Mr. Blanchard?"

"Yes. How is he?"

"We've stabilized him, but his condition isn't good. He sustained a couple of broken ribs and a broken femur. We set the leg but the bigger worry is the considerable swelling on his brain."

"Oh no," Maryse said. "How much damage?"

The doctor shook his head. "We have no way of knowing until he's conscious. And we have no way of knowing when that might occur. Certainly not in the next several hours, but anytime after that...hours, days, weeks...we just don't know."

"So we wait," Maryse said, "indefinitely?"

"No," the doctor said. "When I spoke to the FBI agent who's handling this case, he informed me that Mr. Blanchard left specific instructions concerning life support. If there's no change in his condition within thirty days, we'll remove him from support."

Maryse's eyes filled with tears and Mildred placed her arm around her and squeezed. "Can he survive without support?"

The doctor shook his head. "In his current condition, it's highly unlikely, but if he improves in the next few days, he might be able to. However, there is always the possibility that he won't regain consciousness."

"Oh my God." Maryse swayed a bit and Jadyn saw Mildred's arm tighten on her shoulders to keep her steady.

"I'm sorry I don't have better news," the doctor said, "but I want you prepared for the worst-case scenario."

"Of course," Luc said. "Thank you."

The doctor gave them a nod and left. Luc leaned over to kiss Maryse's ear and whispered something to her that Jadyn couldn't hear. She looked over at Colt, who inclined his head toward a vacant corner in the lobby. She backed away from the emotional scene and joined him in the corner.

"Trying to expand your jurisdiction?" Colt asked, but Jadyn could tell he was making an attempt to lighten the mood.

Jadyn shook her head. "I don't think I want any part of whatever this is, but given that Maryse is my cousin and Raissa and Zach are important to her and Mildred, I wouldn't stay out of it if I thought there was something I could do."

"Good, because the FBI will run this investigation, and they probably won't even give me information, much less let me participate. And without a local involved, I don't know how far they'll get, especially if they start questioning residents."

Jadyn frowned. "So what do you want me to do? I have even less jurisdiction than you do."

"Not necessarily."

"How's that?"

"Mill Highway runs right through the game preserve, and if I understood the location right from Luc, Zach was found in a protected section. That gives you the right to be in that area regardless of what the FBI wants."

"I thought Luc said that search-and-rescue dogs were on the way. Those bloodhounds will be able to find her a lot quicker than me."

Colt shook his head. "There's a million channels back in that swamp. If she got in a boat…"

Jadyn blew out a breath. She'd been slowly exploring the swamps and drafting maps of the bayous and channels, but it was like a mass of spiderwebs. With a boat, you could quite literally go from Mudbug to Minnesota.

"So if we determine that she's somewhere in the swamp, I can search for Raissa, and the FBI can't stop me," she said finally. "That would be more helpful if I had a clue about these swamps, but with my limited knowledge of the area, I won't be of much use, and even though she'd normally be the best person to ask, I don't think Maryse should take on such a task right now."

"No, but you could hire a contractor—you know, a temporary employee to help you get things sorted out from the lapse when Mudbug didn't have a game warden."

"I see," she said, starting to catch on to where Colt was headed. "And I don't suppose you know of someone who'd be interested in such a temporary job?"

"It so happens that I have a bunch of accrued vacation. And I've been stomping around those swamps since I was a boy..."

Jadyn felt her pulse quicken. It was an ideal plan, except for the part where she was alone in the swamp all day with Colt Bertrand. Sure, they'd faced death together, but no matter how hard she tried, she couldn't seem to completely relax around him.

It's because you're attracted to him and don't like to admit it.

"Let me see what's required as far as paperwork goes," she said, brushing her thought aside. "I'll give you a call later as soon as I figure it all out."

"Great. Search-and-rescue will have the hounds out today. If Raissa is anywhere in the area, they'll be able to track her unless she crossed water."

"And if they drove off with her in the car?"

Colt locked his eyes on hers. "Then we've got an even bigger problem. This highway dead-ends in Mudbug, so if they were moving west, there's only one place they were headed."

"And if they went east, they could be anywhere."

"Yeah. First thing we need to try to do is narrow things down. I'll hit up the FBI search party and pitch my local knowledge—see if they'll let me tag along. If they don't find her, at least we'll have a better idea of where to start looking."

"Sounds good."

"There's a diner about thirty minutes down the highway from where Zach was found. It's a long shot and the feds will probably be all over it today, but I might head over there tomorrow and see if anyone saw anything."

"The day staff isn't likely to be the same as the night."

"Yeah, but they'll know who the night staff were and where they live. I'll give you a call tomorrow if you're interested in going."

"Okay."

Luc motioned to Colt and he gave her a nod before heading back across the lobby. Jadyn's mind worked to process all the information she had about Raissa's disappearance, but no matter where she started, the result was never good for Raissa. The fact that they'd struck Zach with a vehicle and left him for dead told her they had no compunction about killing people.

Jadyn hoped Raissa had escaped somewhere in the swamp, but if she had, she was either still running or had collapsed somewhere. If Raissa had been abducted by the people who'd run down Zach, things were much worse. Statistics said if her abductors hadn't killed her already, they would soon. Jadyn figured they had forty-eight hours—max—and that was only if the kidnappers thought Raissa had something they needed.

And if she didn't, Jadyn hoped to God Raissa was creative enough to make it up.

———

COLT CLIMBED into his truck and watched as Jadyn guided a distraught Mildred and Maryse to Maryse's truck. Both women were pale and not even bothering to disguise their immense worry for Raissa. Jadyn glanced at him before slipping into the driver's seat, her concern no less obvious but masked with a look of determination.

As they pulled out of the parking lot, Colt started his truck. He had no doubts about Jadyn's determination to find Raissa. In the short time she'd been in Mudbug, she'd formed hard and fast bonds with Maryse and Mildred. No doubt, she'd do anything to protect those women and that included trying to save someone she'd never even met.

No, he wasn't worried at all about her commitment to the investigation, but he did have doubts about her qualifications to set foot into something like this. Colt had seen sordid and dirty, and the recent happenings in Mudbug had made him seriously question his decision to return to his hometown. He'd thought leaving New Orleans would mean leaving all the worst of criminal offenses behind him, but he'd been wrong. Dead wrong.

But this—the potential kidnapping of a federal agent, attempting to murder another—this was a level of callousness and ego that he'd never believed could exist in such a small place, even after everything that had gone down weeks before. He squeezed the steering wheel, looking out at the sun rising over the line of cypress trees behind the hospital.

What was happening to his town?

He put his truck in drive and headed to the place where Luc had found Zach. With any luck, he wouldn't run into agency politics, and they'd let him stick around.

Colt counted at least fifteen federal vehicles, including two K9 units, lining both sides of Mill Highway as he parked behind one of the vans. He stepped out onto the weedy side of the road and made his way down to where a group of men were gathered. One of the dog handlers was the first man he came upon.

"Who's in charge here?" he asked the handler.

"Special Agent Ross," the handler replied and pointed to a man talking on the phone about twenty feet away.

"Thanks," Colt said.

Ross finished his phone call right as Colt stepped in front of him. His rigid posture screamed former military and he eyed Colt up and down, as if mentally assessing his threat level.

"I'm Colt Bertrand, the local sheriff." He extended his hand.

"Special Agent Thomas Ross," Ross said and gave his hand a firm shake.

"I'm also a personal friend of Zach and Raissa."

Ross nodded. "You been to the hospital?"

"Just came from there."

"How's Zach doing?"

"It's touch and go."

Ross's jaw flexed. "I've never met the agents in person, but their reputation at the bureau precedes them. Rest assured that the bureau is putting every asset available into this investigation. We won't settle for anything short of finding Agent Bordeaux alive and well."

The man's words and demeanor didn't leave any doubt that he fully intended to live up to what he said. Colt had worked with this sort of man before. He'd pursue an angle to the ends of the earth to get an answer and would allow nothing to come between him and a solution. But Colt also knew that no one short of God could promise to return Raissa alive and be 100 percent certain they could live up to those words.

"I'm aware I don't have any jurisdiction here," Colt said, "and I don't want to get in the way, but I know these swamps as well as any other man in Mudbug. I can't track like a hound, but if they indicate a direction, I can tell you what's located in front of you. I can tell you which way all these channels run and where they merge and end."

Ross studied him a couple of seconds, then nodded. "I'm not foolish enough to turn down help from an expert in these parts. Especially not on something this important. Come with me. If you think of anything we need to know along the way, offer it up."

"Thanks," Colt said, as enormous relief swept over him. "I really appreciate you letting me stick around."

"I'd be asking the same if it was my friend out there."

Ross whistled and waved a hand at the men that were milling around. "I want you to split into two groups. Each group will take a dog and proceed in opposite directions along the edge of the highway. Agent Thompson, do you have the clothing?"

"Yes, sir." A young agent standing nearby held up two Baggies with garments inside.

"You're positive the garments belong to Agent Bordeaux and not Agent Blanchard?"

"Unless Agent Blanchard wears women's undergarments, I'm sure."

Ross smiled. "Seems a safe bet. Let the dog take the lead. I want everyone but the handler to case the edges of the swamp, looking for any sign of passage."

One of the men raised a hand. "How far down do we go before circling back?"

"How far is Mudbug?" Ross asked Colt.

"About ten miles to the city limits from here."

Ross nodded. "My team will cover ten miles moving west. Going east, the nearest structure is a diner that's about thirty minutes' drive. I doubt Agent Blanchard chased a car thirty miles, so cover ten miles east then circle around and cover the other side of the highway on the way back until the teams meet up."

"Should we check the swamp?" one of the men asked.

"Yes, but not deeply. If you get an indication from the dog, call me and wait for me to arrive with the other dog before pursuing the lead. Does everyone understand your directive?"

They all nodded.

"I don't think I need to remind any of you that this one is personal. I know we all give 100 percent to our jobs every day, but today, I'm asking you all to double that." He hoisted a backpack over his shoulders. "Let's get to it."

Colt fell in step beside Ross, moving west down the side of the highway. Ross spoke briefly to the dog handler, then headed for the tree line behind the other men. "If you don't mind," he said, "I'd like us to step inside about ten feet. The ground looks softer where the sun doesn't reach. Might be easier to see footprints."

"If there are any," Colt said.

Ross nodded and stepped into the brush. "You got any thoughts about this?"

"Me? Raissa and Zach never talked about their cases."

Ross paused for a second, pinning his gaze on Colt's. "Home office doesn't think this has anything to do with a case."

"They're sure?"

"Seem to be," Ross said and started walking again. "Agents Bordeaux and Blanchard have been working the same case for the last four months. I wasn't involved and can't provide you any details of what I was told, but I will say that the men they were after are safely locked away awaiting federal indictment."

"No fringe elements seeking revenge?"

"It was a small operation and everyone went down in the bust."

Colt rolled that information over in his mind, trying to make sense of it. He'd assumed since he talked to Luc at the hospital that whatever had happened to Zach and Raissa was tied to their work at the bureau, but Ross was telling him straight-out that wasn't the case. It hadn't even crossed his mind that the problem could be a local one, and now that it was front and center, he was even more disturbed than ever.

Realizing he'd never responded to Ross's original question, he shook his head. "If this isn't about the case they were working, I have no idea what to think."

"You got no problem around here with carjackings, that sort of thing?"

"This isn't New Orleans. We've had more than our share of unusual crime in the past year, but nothing like that. Besides which, who would carjack a six-year-old Cadillac? Hell, most every truck in the parish is worth more than that. Some of the bass boats cost half as much as my house."

"So two federal agents just happened to be in the wrong place at the wrong time when a brand-new criminal decided to launch his business?"

Colt's jaw flexed involuntarily. He knew what Ross was implying but damned if he could find an argument to the contrary. The reality was that a hell of a lot of coincidences would have to happen in order for things to play out this way. And if there was one thing Colt had a problem with, it was coincidence.

"I hear what you're saying," Colt said, "but I'm being straight with you. I can't connect this with anything I've run across lately. And if something was going on in my jurisdiction and Raissa and Zach found out about it, they would have told me."

Ross studied him for a couple of seconds, then nodded, apparently satisfied that he was telling the truth. "Well, Sheriff, clearly something is going on here. Whether it's in your jurisdiction or not remains to be seen. But for now, we're moving forward on the assumption that Raissa and Zach walked into the middle of something."

Colt nodded, but the uneasy feeling he'd gotten when he coupled Ross's information with his own didn't subside, even a bit. Granted, Raissa had disappeared outside of his assigned territory, but he didn't think for a minute that made it any less his problem. He fell in step next to Ross, hoping Jadyn was able to figure out how to make him a contractor for the game warden's office.

For the moment, Ross was being polite, but if this search yielded nothing, he'd call for more backup, possibly even the state police, who had far more resources than Colt did. Unfortunately, Colt's experience with the state police had been nothing like his experience with Ross. They pretty much thought anyone but state law enforcement officers were a bunch of unqualified hicks and wouldn't allow or appreciate any interference in their investigation. The last time Colt had inserted himself in state police business, he'd spent two days in jail for the privilege.

He looked over at the highway and watched as the bloodhound strolled on the side of the road, completely relaxed. It wasn't a good sign. If Raissa had exited the road anywhere nearby, that dog would pick up on the scent as if it were right under his nose. If they'd driven out of this area, Colt had no idea what he could do to help. He wouldn't even know where to start.

And if they were in the area, he could only hope that Jadyn could get both of them legitimate access to everywhere they needed to search. As he thought of Jadyn, his mind flashed back to the day before, when he was standing at the front window of the general store as she walked across the street from the hotel to the café. No one had a right to look that good in blue jeans.

He'd hoped his attraction to her had been a temporary thing —something born of near death and high emotions—but he was fooling himself. The fact of the matter was Jadyn St. James was one of the most beautiful women he'd ever seen, and her courage and capability with a gun might just make her the best-looking woman on the face of the earth.

To a man determined to go down in the bachelor hall of fame, Jadyn was kryptonite.

Since the big showdown at the cemetery, he'd managed to put some distance between them. He'd nod or wave if he saw her, as he did with any other Mudbug resident, but he didn't linger to chat and he tried to avoid the café when he knew she was inside. All of which made him feel like a coward, but as of yet, he hadn't figured out another way around it. Not until the feelings went away.

And now, he might be signed up to be alone in the swamps with her every day.

He sighed. If this situation could get any more complicated, he didn't know how.

CHAPTER THREE

MARYSE PULLED open the door to Sabine's new age shop, happy her best friend was back early from her buying trip in New Orleans but dreading the conversation they were about to have. Sabine looked up from the box of candles she was emptying and smiled as she saw Maryse, then her smile began to slip the closer Maryse got to the counter.

"What's wrong?" Sabine asked. "Is it Helena?"

A memory of how her morning had started flashed through Maryse's mind for the first time since the hotel. "There's always something wrong with Helena, but this time, it's something worse."

Sabine's eyes widened and she stopped fussing with the candles. "What's worse than Helena?"

"Maybe we should sit down. Do you have some of that tea... that one you said calms your nerves?"

Sabine reached out to squeeze Maryse's arm. "Okay, now you're scaring me. You hate tea."

"The tea is for you."

Sabine stared at her for several seconds, then gave her a nod. "I put on some water to boil before I started on that box."

They headed toward the back of the shop to the break room. Maryse grabbed a bottled water from the refrigerator while Sabine made her cup of tea. When she'd taken the seat across from Maryse and had her first sip, she put the cup down.

"Please tell me what's wrong," Sabine said.

Maryse took a breath and told Sabine about Raissa and Zach, rushing through the entire story, hoping she could get it all out without crying. Sabine listened silently, then when Maryse finished, she lifted the tea again and took a long sip, her hands shaking as she returned the cup to the table.

"What can I do?" Sabine asked.

Maryse shook her head, certain she looked as miserable as she felt. "That's just it—there's nothing we can do. I mean, pray, but nothing physical. The FBI has search dogs where Zach was found. If there's any trace of Raissa, those dogs will find it."

"So we sit and wait."

"And it's killing me."

"What is Colt doing?"

Maryse shrugged. "He told Luc he'd try to work his way in, but I seriously doubt the FBI is going to let him stroll into the middle of their investigation. Although..."

"What?"

"After the doctor talked to us at the hospital, I saw him talking to Jadyn over in the corner."

"He might have just been bringing her up to speed on all the people and the relationships. With her being new here, he might have assumed she didn't know all the nuances."

Maryse sighed. "True. I guess I'm grasping at straws, thinking there's something one of us can do. I hate sitting."

Sabine reached across the table and squeezed her hand. "So do I, but that's the only job we have right now. As soon as anything changes, we'll be ready for whatever comes our way. I know I'm not the 'real deal' as far as psychics go, and I'm beyond worried, but I'm not getting an overwhelming feeling of doom about this."

"Thanks," Maryse said, attempting to give her best friend an encouraging smile. She didn't believe for a moment that Sabine's feeling meant a thing. More likely, Sabine didn't want to think about anything bad happening to Raissa and her feelings were following suit. But if it gave her comfort, then she was welcome to her thoughts. As for herself, Maryse preferred to deal with the real.

Life held less disappointment that way.

"I probably shouldn't even ask," Sabine said, "but how are things going with Helena?"

"You probably shouldn't ask, especially after this morning."

"Uh-oh. Save the story for a better time, then." Sabine frowned. "I wondered specifically if she's said anything more about why she's back."

"No. I've asked some questions, but she's sticking hard and fast to that story about pissing God off. Short of a better explanation, I'm inclined to believe it's the truth. I'm sure she's capable."

"Yes, well, I'm not going to disagree with you on that point, but I still think God would have a better skill set than the rest of us for dealing with people like Helena."

"You think she's lying?"

"No, not necessarily. But I don't think she's telling us everything."

Maryse frowned. "You think she's back for a specific reason?"

"I've been thinking a lot about it ever since she returned, and ultimately, yes, I think she's here for a specific reason. I also think she knows what that reason is."

"Why wouldn't she tell us? She's never short on words."

Sabine tapped her cup. "Maybe she doesn't want to scare us. Or maybe it's something she needs to do for her own growth and doesn't want to admit it." She shook her head. "I can't put my finger on it, but I'm certain she's holding something back."

Maryse took a big drink of water, what little bit of worry she had left now taken up by Sabine's words. If Helena was keeping a secret, it could only be a bad one.

Really, really bad.

———

COLT DRAGGED himself into the sheriff's department late that evening, more frustrated and tired than he remembered being in years. He'd spent seven hours with the FBI, searching the swamp on both sides of the highway, and they hadn't turned up so much as a footprint. The dogs never gave an indication that Raissa had entered the swamp, and his own observations of the turf and foliage had led to the same conclusion.

He grabbed a bottled water from the small refrigerator next to the filing cabinet and took a long drink as he stared out the side window at the bayou behind the building. As the cold liquid burned his throat and settled like lead in his stomach, he slammed the bottle down on a nearby table.

"I guess you didn't find anything," Shirley, the daytime dispatcher, said.

"Not one damned thing," he said as he turned to look at her.

Normally, Colt tried not to curse around Shirley, a hard-core Southern Baptist, but this time, she didn't so much as lift an eyebrow, much less suggest he use better language as she usually did.

"What did the FBI have to say?"

He shook his head. "Nothing that we didn't already know."

"Do you think that's all to it?"

"Maybe...yeah...I don't know. I mean, I've usually got a good feel for when people are holding back on me, especially other cops, and I think the agent in charge has told me everything he knows."

"But someone above him could be withholding information."

"Exactly. But if they're not telling the man leading the search what he could potentially run into, then there's no way they're going to tell me." He clenched his hand until his fingers dug into his palm. "If the car that hit Zach continued west, there's nowhere else it could have gone but here."

"True, but that car could have turned around at any point and headed right back the way it came. You don't have any reason to believe it did otherwise, do you?"

"No," Colt admitted. He didn't have any concrete reason for believing the car had continued into Mudbug city limits. In fact, it would have made far more sense for it to turn around and head back toward New Orleans. But he had a feeling.

And in his entire law enforcement career, that kind of feeling had never been wrong.

"Have you talked to Jadyn about all this?" Shirley asked.

"Briefly. She brought Mildred and Maryse to the hospital this morning."

Shirley gave an approving nod. "She's a keeper, that one. Reminds me some of Maryse but with better social skills and not so clinical. Doesn't seem a bit like her mother."

"You know her mother?" Colt asked, trying not to sound as curious as he felt.

"Can't say I really know her, but I've met her. One of those former beauty queens—beautiful in physical form, but nasty as they come otherwise. Only took a minute of exposure to know she didn't care about anyone but herself. Makes you wonder how Jadyn did growing up with her, especially as she don't seem the beauty queen type even though she's quite lovely."

"Seems like she did all right." Good heart and good-looking. Maybe she'd gotten the best part of her mother and the rest had come from her father.

"Seems like…well, speak of the devil." Shirley pointed out the front window where Jadyn was crossing the street toward the sheriff's department. Several seconds later, she stepped inside.

"Evening, Shirley," Jadyn said. "How are you today?"

Shirley waved a hand in dismissal. "Same as always and ain't nobody really cares. You go on about your business with the sheriff. I expect that's what you came for."

"Yes, ma'am," Jadyn said and smiled at her before turning toward Colt.

Colt inclined his head toward his office. As he turned, Shirley winked at him, and he held in a groan. Bad enough his attraction to Jadyn had caught him completely unaware and was something he fought daily. The last thing he needed was the town women playing matchmaker.

He opened his office door and waved Jadyn inside, careful not to glance at Shirley as he closed the door. Given her tendency to try to mother him, she might be holding up flash cards. "Have a seat," he said.

Jadyn slipped into a chair in front of his desk as he took his seat behind the desk.

"How did it go today?" she asked.

"Not so good," he said and filled her in on the dismal search results.

The tiny bit of hope she'd been wearing when she walked into his office slipped away to nothing by the time he'd finished his recount of the day.

"Crap," she said when he finished.

He nodded. "I had a similar reaction, but not as polite."

"My original reaction wasn't as polite either. I just didn't verbalize it."

He smiled. "Normally, I prefer it when people see things my way, but this one is a hell of a thing to agree on."

"Yeah. You got any ideas?"

"Not a one. I've been racking my brain, trying to figure out any connection this situation might have with something going on in Mudbug, but I come up empty every time. I know we went through that rough patch a couple weeks ago, but I assure you, Mudbug has been pretty quiet in the twelve months since I've taken the sheriff's job."

"It's not the sort of place you expect high crime to occur, but then..."

She frowned and stared out the back window at the bayou. He held in a sigh. That was the crux of it—but then. If Mudbug were still only a bunch of average hardworking blue-collar folk and the occasional drunk or redneck, then the recent happenings wouldn't have occurred at all. Sooner or later, Colt was going to have to wrap his mind around the fact that the things that happened in New Orleans could also happen in his hometown.

But he wasn't going to get his mind around it today. "Did you check with the state on the contract worker thing?"

She nodded. "I have $750 a month to spend on contract help. If I pay you the minimum of fifteen dollars, that only gives us fifty hours."

"That's no problem. If we have to go that direction, it's not like anyone's watching me punch a time clock. As long as it's legit, that's all that concerns me."

"Then we're good...if we find a reason to need it."

She was still hopeful that a happy ending was forthcoming. He heard it in her voice. Hell, truth be told, he felt the same way. He just wasn't about to count on it.

He reached into his filing drawer and pulled out a stack of folders, then pushed half across the table to Jadyn. "This is every crime committed in Mudbug the past month. I was about to flip through them and see if anything stood out. Why don't you take a look at that stack and when we're done we can trade."

"You're letting me read your case files?" She seemed pleased but a bit surprised.

"Sometimes a second set of eyes sees something different. And that's especially true in your case as you won't have preconceived notions about most of the people in those files."

Jadyn sat back in the chair and opened the first file. Colt reached for the top of his stack but before he could pick up the file, Shirley sounded over his intercom.

"Burton Foster is on line two and he sounds stressed."

Colt frowned as he reached for the phone. The last time Colt could recall Burton, who was retired military, being even remotely perturbed was the day he'd had a heart attack while eating a slice of blackberry pie. And the heart attack wasn't what got him riled. It was the fact that the paramedics wouldn't let him take the rest with him in the ambulance. Rumor had it that Burton had even had fun in the Vietnam conflict. Colt tended to believe the rumors.

"What can I do for you?" Colt asked as he answered.

"There's a boat done sank at the front of Boudreaux's Pond," Burton said. "It's blocking the whole entrance, and red snapper are biting."

Colt held in a sigh. Really? All that worry over fish?

"Damn thing is just under the surface," Burton continued. "I would have tore up my boat something awful if I'd gone through there at my normal clip. Funny thing, too, the top of it's black. Who paints their boat black?"

Colt stiffened and clenched the phone. "Stay right there. I'm on my way."

He dropped the phone back in the cradle and jumped out of his seat. "Come on."

Jadyn popped up out of her chair and put the files on his desk. "What's wrong?"

He opened the cabinet behind him and pulled out scuba gear. "There's something with a black top submerged in Boudreaux's Pond."

Jadyn sucked in a breath.

"Don't assume anything," he said as he caught her expression. "Until we know differently, we proceed as if someone painted his boat black."

She gave him a single nod and took one of the tanks. He hurried out of his office, striding past Shirley so fast she jumped up from her desk.

"Unless it's an emergency," he said as he reached for the front door, "hold all my calls."

He rushed outside, Jadyn following close behind.

As he pulled away from the sheriff's department, he tried to come up with another explanation for what he was on his way to see. Any explanation that didn't include Raissa in that car at the bottom of Boudreaux's Pond.

But no matter how hard he tried, nothing reasonable came.

———

JADYN HELD the scuba mask with one hand and clutched her seat belt with the other as Colt's truck bounced down what could most charitably be called a trail. This was one of the few times she would have welcomed a million thoughts running through her mind, but instead, she had only one. A really bad one.

Colt stared straight ahead, his hands clenching the steering wheel so hard his knuckles were white. He'd been completely silent the entire ten minutes of the drive and Jadyn wished he'd say something...anything. Hell, at this point, she'd even settle for a sneeze to break the uncomfortable silence.

"Does this road go all the way to the pond?" she asked.

"It ends about twenty yards short of the place we want, so if it is a car, then it went off-roading for a good clip. But driving there is quicker than taking the boat. That pond isn't exactly a direct shot down the channels."

"How will we get the...umm, submerged object out?"

"We won't. At least not yet. I want to assess the situation underwater first, then I'll see what kind of equipment we can get back there. I haven't been there in quite some time. I'm not sure what the undergrowth looks like or if the channel has narrowed."

Assess the situation underwater.

The words repeated over and over in her head. They sounded so innocuous, but the literal translation went more like "We need to see if it's a car and if there's a body in it."

He looked over at her. "I just assumed you know how to dive?"

"I do. You never know..."

In north Louisiana she hadn't covered near the span of water that she did in Mudbug, but the need for water recovery was always a possibility, so she'd gotten her certification years ago. Several times, she'd dove on vacation—beautiful, tropical waters with brightly striped fish and coral reefs that looked like a coloring box.

This would be her first dive as part of her job.

Colt slowed and she scanned the brush in front of them. No sign of the trail remained, but Jadyn's chest tightened when she saw the broken trees and scattered brush with two clear tire tracks running through it. Colt's gaze immediately locked on the tire tracks and he frowned.

One question answered, but not the answer they were hoping for.

Colt rolled to a stop at the end of the trail, and they grabbed their gear.

"This way," he said.

She fell in step behind him as he pushed a broken sapling aside and hurried into the brush.

Jadyn expected the density of the foliage to decline as they approached the water and was surprised when she stepped out of the thick underbrush and found herself standing right at the edge of the bayou.

"Careful," Colt said. "The edge of the bank is sandy and could easily give. Just inch along the side here until we get to where there's more bank."

She stepped lightly behind him until they reached hard-packed mud and weeds. A tall, thin man with silver hair stood next to the pond, checking his watch. Jadyn glanced upstream and saw a bass boat tied off to the bank just before the entrance to the pond. As they approached, the man stuck out his hand to Colt.

"Made good time, Sheriff," he said, then looked at Jadyn.

"This is Jadyn St. James," Colt said. "She's the new game warden."

The man looked her up and down, then shook his head. "Don't know what the world is coming to. Wouldn't you rather be home having babies or something?"

Colt closed his eyes and rubbed his forehead, probably waiting for the explosion he thought was coming. He was wrong. Jadyn knew this man. He existed in every small town across the nation. And nothing he said could ruffle her feathers.

"Would you rather be home having babies?" Jadyn asked.

"'Course not!"

"Then why do you assume I would? I got news for you, old-timer, a set of ovaries does not automatically make a woman desire the sound of screaming infants."

Burton looked over at Colt. "Got a mouth on her, doesn't she?"

Colt glanced at her firearm. "That's not all she has on her. You might want to check a calendar. Women have been making a go of it on their own for quite a while now."

"Don't care if it's been a thousand years," Burton said. "I still ain't got to like it."

"How about you show us the boat," Colt said, clearly trying to navigate away from the current conversation.

"This way. Hell."

Jadyn didn't bother to hold in her smile as they followed Burton down the bank. She stopped next to Colt where a small channel fed into the pond. About ten feet from the edge of the water she could see the top of something large and black, a couple of inches below the surface. It didn't look anything like the top of the boats that Jadyn had seen, but it looked exactly like the top of a car.

"Can't be that deep if we can see the top."

"No," Colt agreed, "but the water's murky, so might take some time to inspect. And it's good he found it now because in a couple of hours, the top won't be visible from the surface. Something that heavy will sink fast in the mud. Suit up and let's take a closer look. Mr. Foster, would you mind waiting here while we dive?"

Burton gave him a derisive look. "You never leave a man in the field."

"Of course not." Colt reached into his duffel bag for two underwater flashlights and handed one to Jadyn. "I'll check inside. You check the rear for a license plate number."

She wanted to argue. Wanted to tell him that she was perfectly capable of peering into that car even though it might mean finding Raissa inside. But she knew if she opened her mouth, he'd know she was lying. The truth was she was scared as hell about what might be inside that car. Scared as hell that she'd have to go back to the hotel and tell Mildred and Maryse that they'd never see their friend again. At least not alive.

"Okay," she said and took the flashlight. She checked the pressure on her tank, and followed him to the edge of the pond where she drew up short. "What about alligators?"

He scanned the banks. "Always a possibility, but I don't see any signs. They're probably spooked out of the area for a while."

She wanted to ask what the probability of "probably" was or the exact definition of "for a while" but knew it wouldn't do any good. If Colt knew more, he would have said so and likely he would have insisted she wait on the bank. Not that she would have listened. Technically, the pond was her jurisdiction, and no way was she going to play the little woman and let the big, strong man handle her job. The state paid her to work and by God, that's what she intended to do. Regardless of what the job entailed or how Burton Foster thought she ought to be spending her time.

She waded into the water with Colt as he felt down the side of the car.

"Looks like this is the back," he said, pointing to the side closest to the bank.

"I'll check the plate." Jadyn placed the regulator in her mouth and took a test breath before sinking below the surface.

The water was so murky, it was impossible to see more than a foot in front of her even with the spotlight. She used the side of the car to guide her around the corner to the back, shining her light down the back bumper. When she got to the flat spot where the license plate should have been, only a black space stared back at her.

Damn.

She started to surface, but changed her mind. Maybe some form of identification existed inside the car. Colt was checking the car from the driver's side so she swam around the back to the passenger's side. As she approached the side windows, she could see the dim glow from Colt's flashlight. She felt down the side of the car and realized the passenger side window was rolled down.

Her pulse ticked up a notch as she lifted the flashlight to shine it inside. The light illuminated the passenger seat and relief coursed through her when she saw it was empty. She slid through the window a bit to check the backseat and felt an uptick of hope when it was also clear.

Colt's light had vanished when she went in the window and she glanced around, trying to figure out where he'd gone. Maybe he'd surfaced for some reason. She pushed back a bit and directed her light at the front dashboard. Maybe some paperwork was in the glove compartment. She pulled the compartment open and plastic packet from inside. Everything was probably soaked, but there was always a chance she'd be able to get something off of it.

Deciding she'd gained everything she could in her current position, she surfaced. Her mask fogged over as soon as her head popped out of the water and she reached up with her free hand to lift it. Colt was exiting the water and looked back as he heard her breach the surface.

She held up the packet. "The license plate was gone, but I pulled this out of the glove compartment. We might be able to get something off of the papers inside if they're not completely soaked."

"License plate?" Burton stared at her as if she'd just reported finding an alien spaceship in the pond.

"It's not a boat," Colt explained. "It's a car. Someone probably wedged a stick into the accelerator then popped it in drive."

Burton's eyes widened. "What the hell?"

"I can't tell you how relieved I was to see the car was empty," Jadyn said as she stepped on the bank beside Colt.

He frowned. "We're not in the clear yet. I was just going back to my truck for a crowbar."

Jadyn froze and she sucked in a breath. The trunk. How could she have forgotten the trunk?

Because bodies in trunks are not something a degree in environmental science covers.

She watched as Colt retrieved a crowbar from the toolbox in the back of his truck and made his way back into the water.

"What are you doing with that crowbar?" Burton stood at the edge of the pond, alternating staring at Colt and peering into the pond at the car.

"I need to pop the trunk. Make sure there's nothing inside."

Burton's eyes widened. "You think someone's in that trunk?"

"That's not what I said."

"You didn't have to. What the hell is going on here? There's something you ain't telling me about all this."

"Later," Colt said and looked over Jadyn. "I'm going to need two hands for this. Can you light up the back?"

Jadyn nodded and tried to swallow, but the lump in her throat was so big it seemed to be choking her. She took a couple steps up the bank and placed the packet on the edge of a rock. As she made her way back down the bank, she pulled her mask on, popped her regulator in her mouth, then gave Colt a thumbs-up. He nodded and walked into the pond until he disappeared below the surface. Jadyn said a silent prayer and followed him into the murky depths.

As she approached the rear of the car, Colt's spotlight created an eerie glow in the water surrounding her. Algae and who knew what else floated in tiny pieces around her, minnows darting away as she moved through the water. When she drew up next to Colt, she tapped his arm and he handed her his spotlight.

She directed the light at the center of the car's rear and watched as Colt stuck the crowbar underneath the trunk. Her heartbeat pounded in her chest, then echoed through her ears with a whooshing sound. He shoved the crowbar down but the trunk didn't budge. He turned a bit to the side for better leverage and shoved the crowbar down once more.

At first, Jadyn thought it was another failed attempt, then she realized the trunk lid had crept up an inch but was being held in place by the tide. As Colt reached for the lid, she tightened her grip on the spotlight until her hand ached. Every inch the trunk moved seemed to match a heartbeat until it was wide enough to peer inside. The very back appeared empty, so she moved closer to illuminate the far depths of the trunk.

When she saw nothing but water between her and the backseat of the car, she released the breath she hadn't realized she'd been holding. She sucked in air through the regulator, and the rush of oxygen made her dizzy for a couple of seconds. She felt Colt tap her shoulder and looked over to see him pointing up.

She nodded and pushed off the muddy bottom toward the surface, tearing the mask and regulator off as soon as she breached the surface.

"Anything?" Burton yelled from the bank.

"It's empty," Jadyn replied.

Burton's relief was apparent. "Thank the Lord for that."

Colt surfaced a second later. "Let's see if we can get anything off those papers."

"Crap," Jadyn said as they walked up the bank. "I didn't even think to look at the make of the car."

"I did," Colt said.

"And?"

"It's a Cadillac DTS."

She froze. "Like Raissa and Zach's?"

Colt paused. "I don't know Cadillacs very well, so I can't be certain about the year, but yeah, it looks like theirs. There were also a couple bullet holes in the back windshield."

Jadyn stared after him a couple of seconds before scrambling up the bank behind him. He stopped to talk with Burton, but she didn't pay any attention to the conversation. She looked back at the pond, already unable to see the top of the car any longer.

Nothing made sense. Too many pieces were missing.

And the worst part was, she had to return to the hotel without a single answer.

CHAPTER FOUR

COLT HURRIED into the sheriff's department, greeting Eugenia, the night dispatcher, without even slowing. Jadyn practically jogged behind him, trying to keep up, but he was too anxious to slow his pace. When he hurried into the restroom, Jadyn slid to a stop in front of the door. He pulled a blow-dryer out of the bathroom cabinet and motioned her to his office.

He plugged in the blow-dryer and shoved everything on his desk to one side, then motioned to Jadyn for the packet. He placed it in the middle of the desk and pointed the dryer at the flap. When the flap separated from the rest of the packet, he directed the air inside until he was able to shake the papers inside onto the desk.

He glanced up at Jadyn, who inched closer to the desk, then directed the dryer at the papers. A few minutes later, the papers started to curl a bit, separating from each other. He flipped the stack over and attacked it from the other side until he was able to pull the top paper away from the stack without damaging it.

They both leaned forward to see the blurry ink.

Coupons.

It was a discount coupon printed off a computer.

Colt worked on the remaining papers, but they were all sales ads or discount rates on common items like laptops or cameras. Not a single one of them indicated who might have printed them.

Jadyn stared at the document for several seconds, then sank into a chair. "So we still don't know for sure."

Colt shook his head. "Not for sure, but I'm willing to bet that's Raissa's car. Those tread marks through the swamp were recent and the car couldn't have been there long or it would have sunk much lower. There were bullet holes in the back windshield. The odds are seriously against any other explanation."

"Then what the hell is going on here?"

Colt shook his head. "I can't put together a scenario that works with all the elements we're aware of. Maybe Zach was hit by another vehicle while he was firing at their car, but if it was accidental, then why hasn't the driver of the other vehicle come forward? And if they ditched the car, they either got what they wanted out of it or it wasn't the car they were after in the first place. But what does someone want with Raissa?"

The even worse question in his mind was "what were they doing to her" but he didn't even want to say the words out loud. He hoped to God that if someone was holding Raissa hostage, it was to use her as a bargaining chip, and that they understood that harming her would bring the FBI down on them like a hurricane.

"Zach wouldn't have fired if Raissa was in the car, right?"

Colt considered this for a minute. "The shots were all concentrated on the driver's side of the car. If he thought he could make the shot—take out the driver in order to stop the car—he might have tried it. If it had been someone I cared about in that car, I would have."

"The passenger window was open. Is it possible..."

"I don't think she could have been thrown out when the car hit the water if that's what you mean, but it's possible that the body was dumped before that."

"But there's no good reason to dump the body separately from the car, is there?"

"Not that I can think of."

"Then I'm going to keep believing that Raissa is alive somewhere."

Colt nodded, trying not to think about all the things that could be happening to her as he sat at his desk, without a clue as to where to start looking. "Agent Ross and a couple of his men took rooms at the hotel. We better head down there and tell them what we found."

"What about the car?"

"Technically, it's their jurisdiction now. The feds have better equipment than us. Let them get it out. There's nothing to see anyway."

Nothing he hadn't already seen.

———

AGENT ROSS HAD CROPPED hair and the stiff posture that Jadyn recognized as former military. With her, Colt, Ross, and two other FBI agents all standing in Ross's hotel room, the combination of the men and the testosterone level made Jadyn feet a bit claustrophobic. On the positive side, Ross didn't so much as blink when Colt introduced her as the game warden and that was definitely points in his favor.

"Why didn't you notify me immediately when you got the call from this Burton?" Ross asked, looking slightly perturbed.

"Notify you that a fisherman reported a sunken boat? Do you know how many times a week that happens here?"

Ross's jaw flexed. He knew Colt had skirted the fed's jurisdiction, but there wasn't a thing he could do about it given the circumstances. "You should have called me in as soon as you realized it was a car."

"Maybe, but if there had been anything of value to retrieve, it might have been damaged by the time you arrived, and likely, the gators that usually occupy that pond would have made their way back. Things are rarely black and white in the swamps. I've got more to consider than jurisdiction."

A flush crept up Ross's face and Jadyn inwardly cringed, wondering how much their failure to contact the agent in the beginning was going to affect what they could do in the future.

"Fine," Ross said finally, "but from now on, you stay out of the swamps. Stick to your jurisdiction. I don't want to hear that either of you were anywhere near that pond again. Are we clear?"

"No sir, we are not," Jadyn said. "You're free to tell the sheriff anything you'd like, but you have no right to tell me I can't do my job. And my job is these swamps...all of the swamps. If I've got cause to be in the area, you can bet I will be."

Ross's eyes widened and he glared at her. "If you insist on pushing, I can take this to the state."

"Then I suggest you start now. As efficient as they are, you can expect a return call from my superiors in a week or so."

"Fine. Is that all you have for me?" Ross asked, clearly done with the conversation.

Colt handed him a piece of paper. "That's directions to the pond. You may be able to get a tow truck down the bank using some support planks."

Ross snatched the paper from Colt's hand and opened the door. Jadyn and Colt trailed out without so much as a good-bye. Ross slammed the door behind them.

"I thought you said he was okay," Jadyn said as they headed down the hallway.

"He was before, but this was bound to happen sooner or later," Colt said. "I'm sure his boss is coming down on him, especially since the dogs didn't find anything today. Emotions are running high, and if Ross gets them answers, he'll probably get a big promotion out of it."

"And if he doesn't?"

He shook his head. "He better be happy with the job he has now."

"Are all the law enforcement agencies that brutal?"

"The ones I'm familiar with, it's pretty standard."

"I wonder how Luc handles it. He seems well adjusted."

"According to the rumor mill, Luc is pretty much a legend in the DEA. He doesn't ever talk about his work, but the conviction rate on his cases is double the agency average."

"You think he'll be running the DEA one day?"

"Doubt it. I think Luc likes what he does. Sitting behind a desk would be a slow death."

"I get that," Jadyn said as they stepped into the lobby.

Mildred was at the front desk and gave them a quick nod before hustling off down the hall. Jadyn briefly wondered what was that pressing at 9:00 p.m. but figured she'd find out soon enough.

"So what now?" she asked.

Colt ran one hand through his hair, looking incredibly frustrated. "Despite the edict from Ross, I think we should search the area."

"You think someone's holding her nearby?"

"She's somewhere. Might as well start looking where we know they were. There's any number of fishing camps—shacks mostly—that someone could hole up in if they were looking to."

"What time?"

"Sun's up at six. I want to be in the bayou before Ross gets there, so say five thirty."

"I'll meet you at the dock. Anything special I need to bring?"

"Binoculars, and plenty of extra ammo...just in case."

Jadyn nodded. *Just in case.*

Colt exited the hotel and she watched him through the plate-glass front as he walked down the sidewalk. The maps of the bayous that she'd started on last week all rolled through her mind as she tried to place the location of the car in relation to the channels she'd already charted.

"You're thinking awfully deep there," Mildred's voice sounded behind her.

She turned around to face the hotel owner and sighed. "I have a lot to think about."

Mildred nodded. "We all do. I just put on a pot of coffee. Shirley called and told me about the car. You want to bring me up to speed on everything else?"

"Of course," Jadyn said, immediately feeling guilty. She'd been so focused on the events of the day and the plans for tomorrow that she'd completely forgotten she hadn't had a chance to fill Mildred and Maryse in on anything. They were probably both ready to explode.

"Can we call Maryse?" Jadyn asked as she trailed behind Mildred to her office.

"Ha," Mildred said. "If we don't she might shoot us. She's probably been staring at her phone all day."

Jadyn took a seat in Mildred's office and the hotel owner returned a minute later with a coffeepot and a tray of cups and sweetener. Jadyn had just finished pouring two cups when Helena popped through the wall and took a seat next to Jadyn.

Mildred gave her a disapproving look. "Where have you been all day?"

"What do you care? Seemed you guys wanted me scarce this morning, so I got scarce."

"No," Mildred corrected, "we wanted you to stop stealing food, and that's not the reason you fled. Later on, you and I are going to have a talk about the cat and Maryse's daddy's ashes."

Helena's eyes widened, probably putting together the gunfire and broken urn. "Uh-oh."

"You got that right," Mildred said. "A long, unpleasant talk. The only reason I haven't been looking for you sooner is because we've got a bigger emergency than you."

Helena sobered. "I heard about Zach and Raissa down at the beauty shop. I hitched a ride with a trucker and waited for the search team to return to their cars. I know they didn't find anything. And I heard you guys talking to that Agent Ross. What an ass he is."

"I didn't see you," Jadyn said.

"I was hiding in the bathroom. I heard you and Colt coming up the stairs and thought you were finally going to get some of that hot action, but then you went up another flight, so I followed you."

Jadyn studied Helena for a minute. "I don't suppose you thought to stick around after Colt and I left to see what the agents said?"

"Of course I did. Do you take me for a fool?"

"I'm not touching that," Jadyn said. "What did they say?"

"That Ross did some cussing and stomping, talking about how Colt was a jackass and you were a stone bitch. How his entire career was riding on this case and he wasn't about to let two small-town amateurs blow it for him."

"That's exactly what Colt figured his problem was," Jadyn said.

"Don't worry," Helena said. "I put shampoo in his contact lens solution."

Mildred coughed and Jadyn could tell she was holding in a laugh. She didn't even bother to hold back her grin. "Normally," she said, "I would say that wasn't nice, but in this case, I heartily approve."

Helena brightened. "I could do more. There's this trick with Preparation H—"

"No!" Mildred and Jadyn both sounded off at once.

"But it would be very helpful," Jadyn said, "if you would find out what their plans are for tomorrow."

"I already know. They're going to get a tow truck down to the pond and pull the car out, then their forensics team is going to go over every inch of it, because no way could you and Colt have done a thorough job with it submerged in the pond."

"In theory," Jadyn said, "I'd agree with him, but the fact is, the car's empty. And it's not like they're going to get any DNA evidence out of it now. But whatever. At least they'll get the VIN and we'll know for certain it's Raissa's. And if Ross is distracted with the car, he won't notice what Colt and I are doing."

"Good point," Mildred said. "Are you ready to call Maryse?"

Jadyn nodded.

Mildred pointed a finger at Helena. "You need to stick around and listen to this. I don't want to have to update you later on."

"I don't suppose you could whip up a quick banana pudding?" Helena asked.

"No, I can not." Mildred put the phone on speaker and dialed Maryse, who answered before the first ring even finished.

Jadyn proceeded to recap everything that had happened that day. She figured they'd already heard some of it through the Mudbug grapevine, but all three women listened without interruption. Mildred's worried expression, however, told Jadyn everything the older woman was thinking.

"You're going to start checking camps tomorrow morning?" Maryse asked.

"Yes," Jadyn said. "Colt thinks if someone's holding Raissa nearby, one of the camps is the most likely location."

"I agree," Maryse said, "but there's so many."

"Can we cover them all in a day?"

"No way. Not every one in the game preserve, anyway. You

might be able to cover three-quarters. If you move fast and work the channels efficiently."

"Then that will have to do," Jadyn said. "We'll cover the rest the next day."

"Is there anything we can do?" Mildred asked. "I feel so useless and guilty just sitting here, but for the life of me, I can't think of anything I could do to help."

"Helena can help by shadowing the FBI, particularly Agent Ross."

Helena shook her head. "I was married to an asshole for over three decades. I've had enough of that to last me a lifetime."

Jadyn narrowed her eyes at Helena. "Mildred told me all about your husband, so I know you could have paid him to go away but were too cheap or stubborn to purchase a better life. But the point is, this isn't about you. It's about finding Raissa and you owing Maryse huge…enormously, as a matter of fact. So you'll follow Ross, even into the restroom, just in case he says something that the FBI has been keeping from us."

Helena slumped down in the chair and crossed her arms over her chest. "Guess I can see how you and Maryse are related. You're both rude."

"Never claimed otherwise."

"I suppose I could have the rooms bugged," Mildred said, "but with the rate things get done in this town, Ross would be retired before I got anyone out here to do it."

"For a change," Jadyn said, "I'd like to try to stay on the right side of the law. I'm all for bending the ever-living hell out of it, but I don't think our own personal Watergate is a good move at this point. It's not like anyone can prosecute us for having a ghost spy on them."

"True," Mildred agreed, "but surely there's something I can do besides sit here and worry. It's giving me wrinkles and I've already eaten an entire bag of Oreos this afternoon."

"You had Oreos?" Helena asked.

"Forget the Oreos." Jadyn waved a hand at the ghost. "There *is* the diner up the highway from where Zach was found. Colt figured the feds would be all over it today, but we were going to hit it tomorrow on the off chance that someone says something."

"I know the place," Maryse said. "Lots of truckers and shrimpers. A little rough but the chicken-fried steak is decent."

"I like chicken-fried steak," Helena said.

Jadyn counted to three, then looked at Mildred. "Colt and I will be in the swamp all day tomorrow, but there's nothing stopping us from going to the diner tonight."

"But we're not cops," Maryse said. "We don't have any right to question people."

"No, but we're friends of the victim, and people may be more willing to talk to us than to the police."

"She's right," Mildred said. "Play up the worried friend angle to the hilt and lips tend to loosen a bit."

"I think it's a good idea," Maryse said, "but I don't think all three of us should go. That might seem overwhelming. But you and Mildred should do it."

"Why me?" Jadyn asked. "Wouldn't you rather go with Mildred?"

"Yes," Maryse said, "but I'm not the best choice. I suck at reading people and aside from science, I don't have a logical bone in my body. If they know anything at all, you'll be able to get it out of them, and figure out what it means."

Jadyn felt her face flush slightly at the compliment.

"Besides which," Maryse continued, "if I'm going to get into hot water with Luc over sticking my nose into this, then I'd rather it be when I'm sure I can make something happen."

"Okay," Jadyn said, "then Mildred and I will go to the diner and see if we can drum up some information. We'll call you as soon as we leave."

"Great," Maryse said. "And Jadyn...thanks."

"You ready?" Jadyn looked over at Mildred, who frowned.

"I was thinking," Mildred said, "we may be able to get more out of people if we said Raissa was family. We wouldn't really be lying. She may not be my blood but I love the girl like she is."

Jadyn considered the potential pitfalls. "Any chance the diner employees will know you and your family well enough to call bullshit?"

"I don't think so. Mudbug is the end of the road as far as the highway goes and I know everyone living here. The diner is far enough away that most people working there probably live closer to New Orleans where there's more retail."

"And no one should know me yet," Jadyn said, "so I can be a cousin."

"I like chicken-fried steak," Helena repeated.

"You're not going," Mildred said.

"Actually," Jadyn said, "as much as I hate to admit this, Helena could come in handy."

"See, I'm handy." Helena looked at Jadyn and frowned. "What am I handy with?"

"Not handy 'with' but handy 'for,'" Jadyn said. "Lots of people don't want to get involved with the police on any level. So even if they think Mildred and I are family, they might still clam up. But when we're talking out front, the cooks may whisper in the back, and after we leave, some of them may talk among themselves. That's where you come in."

Helena's expression cleared. "I get it. I'm covert operations."

"Something like that," Jadyn said.

"Will you buy me a chicken-fried steak?"

Jadyn sighed.

COLT HAD NO SOONER TURNED on his shower than his cell phone rang. He looked at the display and held in a curse. It was Eugenia.

"What's up?" he asked.

"Old Man Humphrey called up here all in a snit. The fool says someone stole one of his cars."

"You shouldn't call him 'Old Man Humphrey.'"

"Why the heck not? He was old when I was born and I'm old now. That makes him ancient."

Colt held in a sigh. "Old Man...er, Mr. Humphrey hasn't driven a car in at least a decade."

"Yes, but that hasn't stopped him from piling them up in his yard like an extra on *Sanford and Son*."

"Well, send Deputy Nelson over there."

"Do you think I'd be bothering you if that was an option? Deputy Nelson is tied up at the high school. Bunch of kids smoking weed and drinking beer. A parent caught them and all hell broke loose since everyone's pointing fingers at the mayor's kid as the supplier."

He closed his eyes and groaned.

"If you'd prefer to take over at the school, I can send Deputy Nelson to Humphrey's house."

"No! God no, I wouldn't prefer that. I'm sure I'll be hearing from the mayor soon enough. Deputy Nelson can take a few licks. Tell Humphrey I'm on my way."

He shut off the shower and complained to thin air the entire drive to Old Man Humphrey's house. It was set back a ways in the swamp at the end of a dead-end road. Which was all good news for Mudbug. Eugenia hadn't been exaggerating when she likened his place to *Sanford and Son*. It looked like the place cars came to die.

The entire front lawn was littered with automobiles—trucks, cars, convertibles, hardtops, sedans, and sports cars.

Stan Humphrey was standing on the front porch holding a

whiskey glass and smoking a cigar, apparently intent on openly defying death. He frowned when Colt got out of his truck.

"Took you long enough," he complained. "A man could die before law enforcement gets around to working in this town."

A man who should have been dead years ago shouldn't be so picky.

"It's been a busy day."

"Your shortage of help ain't my concern, but what is my concern is my missing car."

Colt held in a sigh. "That's what I'm here for. You want to tell me what happened?"

Stan threw his arms up in the air, sloshing whiskey across his front porch. "I done told the dispatcher everything I know. The car was here. Now it's not."

"When was the last time you saw the car?"

"When I came home from church. Good sermon today. All about how being lazy is a sin. You should have been there."

Colt glanced upward, wondering why God had seen fit to pile this on top of what had already been an exhausting and disappointing day. "Sir, you couldn't possibly have seen your car after church today because it's Monday."

Stan stared at him for several seconds, then blinked. "Well shit fire and save the matches! You mean I been napping for a whole day?"

"Twenty-four hours is more like a short hibernation than a long nap."

Stan waved a hand in dismissal, his marathon nap clearly of no concern. "No matter. Facts still the same. The car was here when I got home from church."

"Yes, sir, but the amount of time during which the thieves could have taken it is significantly longer."

Stan just stared.

"You know what," Colt said, "never mind. Give me the make and model of the car."

"It was a Cadillac DeVille. Damn fine automobile in her day. Had me a roll in the backseat with Melvina Watkins. Took her virginity, matter of fact. Might have been the best day of my life." He narrowed his eyes at Colt. "That was before I found God, mind you. I don't want you casting any aspersions on my character."

"Of course not. Did the car still run?"

"Can't remember. Probably not, but it might not have needed more than a battery to make it go. I mostly kept it around for sentimental reasons."

Colt glanced around at no less than forty vehicles with flat tires and weeds growing around them and wondered how many of them had a Melvina-in-the-backseat story.

Not wanting to dwell on the matter, he focused on what facts he could drum out of what had to be one of the strangest crimes he'd seen since he returned to Mudbug. At minimum, it would take a battery and air in the tires—assuming they would even hold air—to get one of the cars out of the yard. But more likely, whoever had taken the car had towed it off. If it was even missing, and given that Stan was the only witness, that was looking shaky.

"Where was it parked?"

"Right up front just past the mailbox. You can see the empty spot."

Colt walked to the edge of the lawn and took a look. A large square spot of bare ground sat surrounded by weeds. Tire tracks led through the weeds at the front of the lawn and onto the dirt road. He squatted down and picked up a handful of soil to take a closer look at, but it looked normal. Something had been covering this space or it would be grown over like the rest of the yard, and since he couldn't spot a single green stem anywhere in the dirt, he had to assume that whatever had been here had been moved recently.

Maybe Old Man Humphrey wasn't crazy after all.

He made his way back up to the house, where Stan was lighting another cigar. "Do you have a license plate number for the car?"

"Don't think it had a plate on it. Hadn't been driven in years. Kept it around for sentimental reasons."

"Do you have the title to the car? I need the vehicle identification number in order to identify it as your property once it's found."

"What the hell would I need the title for? Ain't like I'm selling it."

"You can apply for a lost title. But I'm going to need some way to identify the car."

"Title's probably in the house somewhere, but it might take me a bit to find it."

If the inside of the house looked anything like the yard, Indiana Jones probably couldn't find that title, but that wasn't Colt's problem.

"I'll have Deputy Nelson do some asking around tomorrow," Colt said. "If you think of anything else I need to know, give my office a call. I'll be out of pocket for a day or two."

"Those government jobs give you people entirely too much vacation. Always ducking out when you ought to be working."

"I'm not vacationing." *Technically, I am, but not really.* "We've got a missing person...a federal agent and probably kidnapped."

Stan's eyes widened and he stared at Colt for a bit, probably trying to gauge whether he was pulling his leg or not. He must have decided Colt was telling him the truth because he threw his arms in the air again, spilling what remained of his whiskey. "What the hell is this town coming to?"

"I don't know, sir. Have you seen anything out of place around lately? Aside from your missing car?"

Stan shook his head. "Been quiet as far as I know. Who's the agent?"

"Name is Raissa Bordeaux. She moved here last year."

Stan's expression went from incredulous to worried. "I know Raissa. She helped me get a hunting rifle sighted a couple months ago. What the hell are you doing standing here jawing about an old car? Get out there and find that girl." He shook his head. "You young people really need to learn how to prioritize."

"Yes, sir."

Some days, there was just no winning.

CHAPTER FIVE

JADYN PULLED MILDRED'S sedan into the parking lot of Ted's Diner next to three Harley-Davidson motorcycles and looked over at Mildred and Helena. "Does everyone understand the plan?"

Helena rolled her eyes. "You've been rattling about it ad nauseam the entire drive."

Jadyn turned around and looked directly at her. "So you mean even the dead have heard me."

"Low blow," Helena said and stepped through the side of the car.

Jadyn and Mildred climbed out and made their way to the front door. "Scan the room first," Jadyn reminded her, "and if you see anyone who knows you, switch to plan B. I'll follow your lead."

Mildred nodded. "I hope we find out something that helps."

"Me, too."

Jadyn pushed open the door and they walked inside. Where the café in Mudbug was bright and had a homey feel, the diner was dim and the furniture was run-down, giving the whole place a dingy look. Three beefy tattooed men—the only other patrons—

looked up from a table toward the back when they walked inside but then went back to their conversation.

Jadyn was happy to see the bar counter at the front of the restaurant with the serving window directly behind it. It was something she'd hoped to find, as this way, the kitchen staff would be able to hear their conversation. If the kitchen staff started talking among themselves, Helena would be on point to listen in on the conversation.

A red-haired woman who looked fifty but probably wasn't a day over forty walked up to them, a bored expression on her face. "Help you?" she asked.

"Yes, two coffees please," Jadyn said, making a note of her name tag that said "Dee."

As Dee reached for the coffeepot behind her, a head popped up in the food service window and Jadyn did a double take. The person was wearing what could only be construed as a Batgirl mask. Jadyn glanced over at Mildred, who was staring at the masked person, her jaw dropped slightly.

"Helena?" Mildred mouthed.

Given that Dee was inches away from the masked kitchen bandit and hadn't even uttered a peep, Jadyn was certain it was Helena. Either that or Ted hired the oddest set of cooks she'd ever seen. Before Jadyn could reply, the masked bandit gave Jadyn a thumbs-up and a second later, a basket of butter disappeared from the window.

Definitely Helena.

Dee turned around and placed two cups of coffee in front of them. "I ain't seen you before. You passing through?" she asked as she poured.

Mildred glanced at Jadyn, then looked back at the Dee. "Not exactly. We live in Mudbug but we were hoping you could help us with something."

Dee's expression shifted from bored to guarded. "You cops?"

Mildred laughed. "Not hardly."

Dee didn't look completely convinced. "We had enough cops around here today to last a lifetime. Rude, too."

Jadyn laughed. "You and I probably talked to the same person."

Dee narrowed her eyes at Jadyn. "You involved with that missing woman?"

"Not involved," Jadyn said. "Related. She's my cousin. Mildred here is our aunt."

"Oh." Dee's expression softened a bit. "I'm sorry to hear that. You must be really worried."

Mildred sniffed and rubbed her nose with a napkin. "Haven't thought of anything else since I found out this morning. I just can't help thinking what those people may be doing to her and I..."

Mildred's voice broke and Jadyn put her arm around her and gave her a squeeze. "She's going to be fine, Auntie. We have to stay positive."

Dee's face crumpled and Jadyn knew they had roped her in.

Mildred sniffed again and nodded. "I know, but it's so hard when you have to just sit there when you feel like you ought to be doing something."

"I know," Jadyn said and looked back at Dee. "That's why we're here. The cops won't tell us much, so we thought we'd try to get some answers ourselves. We couldn't take sitting in that living room staring at each other any longer."

"Of course not," Dee said.

"A friend told us this diner was up the road from where they think my cousin was kidnapped, so we figured we'd ask if anyone had seen anything. I know it probably seems foolish, but we had to do something."

Dee put her hand on Mildred's. "It's not stupid at all. If it was my family, I'd be raising heaven and hell to get them back."

"Were you working last night?" Jadyn asked.

Dee nodded. "Five 'til one is my usual shift. I saw your cousin last night. Seen her a couple times before."

Jadyn straightened on her stool and Mildred stared at Dee, her eyes wide. Despite her hopes, Jadyn hadn't expected that Zach and Raissa had actually been in the diner.

"You're sure it was her?" Mildred asked.

"Yeah," Dee said. "The cops showed me a picture of them. She's a looker and had polish you don't usually see in here. It was her. They said they found the man but he was hurt."

Mildred nodded. "He's in a coma and it's touch and go, so he's not able to give us any information."

"That sucks."

"Was anyone else with them," Mildred asked, "or did anyone else talk to them?"

Dee shook her head. "They was alone. Sat right here at the counter and had a cup of coffee and slice of pie. Said they were on their way home after working out of town for a bit and needed a little pick-me-up to make the last hour's drive."

"Did they look worried or anything?" Mildred asked.

"Can't say as they did. We chatted a bit about the weather and how striped bass was biting. The guy said he planned on spending the next couple days fishing. She joked that he was gonna spend at least one painting the living room. Seemed normal...you know, a nice couple. What kind of work do they do?"

Because she couldn't see any reason to lie, Jadyn decided the truth was probably easiest. "They're both FBI agents," Jadyn said.

Dee's eyes widened. "No shit? Wow, I would never have figured them for feds. They wasn't stiff or rude or anything like the others."

"They are both very nice and not at all rude unless someone pushes them to it," Mildred said. "Which is why we can't figure out what happened."

"Maybe some of the bad guys they was chasing came after them," Dee said. "I see that sorta thing all the time in movies."

"It's a possibility," Jadyn agreed, "although not a pleasant one."

Dee shook her head. "Ain't no pleasant possibility when a woman's gone missing, unlessin' she runned off herself."

"True," Jadyn agreed.

"So they left here and everything was normal?" Mildred asked. "I mean, I'm sorta glad they had a good moment before all the trouble, but at the same time..."

"You ain't got no answers," Dee said. "Kinda crappy, if you ask me."

"What about other customers?" Jadyn asked. "Anyone been around lately that you didn't know or that looked out of place?"

Dee shook her head. "I can't recall anyone I didn't know coming in for weeks. Last time I can think of was when a fishing tournament was going on. That was about a month ago, though."

"Well then," Mildred said, "I guess that's that."

Dee gave her a sympathetic look. "I'm really sorry I can't help. Your niece was really nice and left a big tip. I sure hope they find her soon."

"Damn it, Marty!" an angry male voice sounded from the kitchen. "I told you that ham sandwich was mine. I don't get paid to fix your supper."

"I didn't touch your sandwich," another man said. "I don't even like ham."

Jadyn glanced over at Mildred and held in a groan.

"Well, it didn't disappear in thin air," the first man continued, "and I know I didn't eat it."

"Maybe you forgot. Your mind has been going downhill ever since you turned fifty."

Dee looked over the serving counter. "If you two are going to fight like five-year-olds, take it out back. No one else should have to listen to that mess."

Dee turned back around. "Do you ladies want anything to eat? I'm kinda hoping not since I just sent the cooks out back, but we do have some incredible apple pie."

Helena the Batgirl's head popped over the counter. "I want pie."

"No, thank you," Mildred said. "We're on a diet."

Dee sighed. "It's the state I live in."

"Excuse me," a man's voice sounded behind them.

They turned around to find the three biker guys standing behind them. Instantly, Jadyn's pulse clicked up a notch.

"We couldn't help overhearing your conversation," the guy said. "What kind of car was your cousin driving?"

"It was a black Cadillac DTS," Jadyn replied.

The man looked back at his two buddies, who both nodded. "I think we saw that car on the side of the highway maybe thirty miles toward Mudbug."

Jadyn's pulse quickened. "What time?"

"About eleven. They had a flat and the man had the trunk open. I figure to change it. There was someone else in the car. We stopped and asked if they needed help, but he said he was good and thanked us, so we went on."

Jadyn pulled a snapshot of Raissa and Zach from her pocket. "Was this the couple you saw?"

The man looked at the photo and nodded. "It was dark but I'm pretty sure that was the guy I saw. We were on our way to visit a buddy in Mudbug but didn't head back until tonight, so I don't know how long they were there."

"Did you see any other vehicles on the highway?" Jadyn asked.

"No, sorry. That stretch of the highway usually isn't busy that late at night. We didn't see any other cars but your cousin's. You said the woman's missing?"

Jadyn nodded. "Someone ran over her husband, and we can only assume they kidnapped her."

The man shook his head. "That's bad news. We got a couple buddies in Mudbug and some other towns nearby. Not all of 'em are into the legal sort of business, if you know what I mean, but I'll ask around and see if they've heard anything."

"I would really appreciate that," Jadyn said and pulled a card from her wallet. "Here's my contact information. Please call any time and thank you."

The man looked at the card, then back at Jadyn and grinned. "Game warden, huh? I knew you looked like a woman who could take care of business. You ever interested in company, look me up at Mike's in Rabbit Creek."

"Uh, yeah," Jadyn said. "If I'm ever in the area, I'll do that."

"Liar," Helena's voice sounded behind her. "Dude looks like Grizzly Adams meets Prisoner Number One."

Mildred coughed. "Thank you," she said. "I really appreciate your trying to help."

"No problem," the man said. "I hope they find her soon."

He and his buddies gave them a nod and left the café.

Jadyn and Mildred turned back around to face Dee. "Well," Jadyn said, "I guess that's all we're going to get, but it's something. At least we know why Zach was found down the highway away from everything."

Mildred nodded. "And I feel better now that we did something. I guess we best head home or neither of us will want to get up for work in the morning."

Dee gave them both a sympathetic smile. "Would you ladies like some coffee for the road?"

"That would be great," Jadyn said.

"And apple pie!" Helena yelled from the back.

"No way," Mildred muttered under her breath.

Jadyn held in a grin. She agreed with the sentiment, but had a feeling they'd both pay for it on the way back to Mudbug. Helena's mouth never ran out of gas.

They collected the coffee and Jadyn slipped a twenty and one of her business cards onto the counter. Dee's eyes widened and she stuffed the money into her apron. "I'll keep asking around. If I hear anything, I'll call."

"We appreciate it," Jadyn said and they headed outside to the car.

As they climbed inside, Jadyn looked back toward the front of the café. "I wonder if the cooks said anything."

"You mean besides arguing over that sandwich Helena stole?"

"Yeah. Besides that."

Mildred shook her head. "We have got to figure out some way to get her under control."

"Don't look at me," Jadyn said. "I'm new to all this, but if you couldn't figure it out last time, I'm not holding out much hope. I mean, what punishment can you come up with for someone who's already dead?

"And therein lies the crux of the matter. You can talk until you're blue in the face, but if she doesn't want to cooperate..."

"We need to get creative. Think outside the box. That exorcism threat is only going to last so long before she calls our bluff. Where is she, anyway? Surely they're not still trading secrets in there."

A second later, Jadyn wished she hadn't asked.

The two cooks walked around the side of the café from the back, smoking cigarettes and looking like they'd gotten past their earlier argument. Just as they rounded the corner to the front of the café, Helena burst through the wall, running for the car and clutching a pie.

Jadyn would have liked to say that the Batgirl mask looked better when the entire costume was in view, but that would have been the lie of the century. The black spandex bodysuit clung to every square inch of Helena's body, identifying rolls in places Jadyn hadn't even known it was possible to have them.

"I'm going to need therapy," Mildred said as Helena changed direction and headed straight for the car.

Jadyn started the car, threw it in reverse, and squealed out of the parking space. The car hadn't even stopped its backward motion before she shifted to drive and took off from the café. Helena ran about ten yards before giving up. Jadyn didn't even want to imagine what the poor cooks were thinking, standing there watching a hovering pie.

"Should we leave her there?" Mildred asked.

"Yes." Jadyn shook her head. "But I probably won't. I need to give the cooks a chance to get back inside before we pick her up."

"You think they'll call the cops?"

"And say what—that an apple pie floated through the wall of the café and hurried down the highway?"

Jadyn slowed down and made a U-turn in the middle of the empty highway, then idled back toward the diner. When she was about a quarter of a mile away, she turned off the headlights. "Watch for cars."

Mildred nodded. "How are we going to see her in the dark, especially with that getup she's got on?"

"Heck if I know. Maybe we can—"

A loud thud sounded in front of them and a second later, something large and black crashed onto the hood and rolled up and over the top of the car. Mildred threw her hands up and screamed. Jadyn stomped on the brakes so hard she almost banged her head on the steering wheel. The two coffees exploded in the cup holder and sprayed all over both of them.

The abrupt stop sent the object on top of the car rolling back down and onto the hood where it came to a heaped stop. The apple pie running down the windshield gave away the black heap. Helena looked up at them, and Jadyn could see her guilty expression, even with the ridiculous mask.

A second later, the air bags deployed.

"Are you all right?" Jadyn asked.

"I just got an unplanned facial," Mildred said, "and my neck may never be the same, but I don't think I'll die. I can't say the same about others. How the hell do you get out of these things?"

"Hold on. I have a pocket knife."

Jadyn pushed against the air bag, trying to move it enough to reach her back pocket. Four years of gymnastics training and two years of yoga were pushed to the very limit, but she finally managed to snag the tiny knife and release her and Mildred from their nylon prison.

Helena was still piled on the hood of the car, not moving, and for a minute, Jadyn worried if it was possible to die twice. Part of her hoped so.

She stepped out of the car and poked Helena with a finger. "You alive?"

"Of course I'm not alive!" Helena shouted. "I've been dead for over a year."

"My bad. Then I need you to get off the hood and into the car so we can get out of here before someone calls the cops."

"I can't move."

"Why not?"

"I think I broke a hip."

Jadyn blew out a breath. "That's not possible. You're dead."

"Now you remember."

Mildred climbed out of the car and looked across the hood. "What's the holdup?"

"Helena thinks she broke a hip."

Mildred put her hands on her hips and glared at the lump. "If you don't get up off that hood, I swear to God I'm going to climb up there with you and strangle the afterlife out of you."

Helena lifted her head up and glared at Jadyn. "You two are cruel."

"You don't know the half of it," Mildred said. "Look what you did to my car. Why can't you just remain transparent?"

Helena rolled over and slid off the front of the hood. Jadyn had turned the headlights on before she climbed out of the car and now, they were like a spotlight on the ghost. It was like something out of a horror movie.

The Batgirl mask was torn on one side, leaving only one eye and bright red lips protruding. The spandex body suit, which had already been stretched beyond intended capacity, had given way in the tumble and now rolls of Helena spilled out of various rips and tears.

"What's wrong?" Helena said when she realized they were staring. She whipped around, apparently thinking their looks of dismay were caused by something behind her.

And gave them a full view of the biggest bodysuit tear of all.

Mildred groaned and lifted her hand over her eyes. "It's a full moon over Mudbug."

Helena grabbed her butt. "I thought I felt a draft."

Jadyn cringed as Helena fingered the tattered suit. "Why are you wearing that in the first place? Didn't getting shot at by Maryse teach you anything about wardrobe selection?"

Helena let out an exasperated sigh. "This was my Batgirl suit. The other one was my scary cat burglar outfit."

"I've got news for you," Mildred said. "They're all scary."

"Can you change into something that covers everything that should be covered and get into the car?" Jadyn asked.

Helena turned around to face them and shrugged. "I suppose so. This suit is shot anyway."

She waved her hands in the air, but nothing happened. "Uh-oh."

"What do you mean, 'uh-oh'?" Jadyn asked, already afraid she knew the answer.

"It's not working," Helena said. "It happens sometimes."

"Hmmmph," Mildred said. "It never seems to happen when you're wearing jeans and a sensible shirt."

"I think I'm stressed," Helena said.

Mildred's eyes widened and Jadyn was convinced if the hotel owner had a gun, she would have fired off a magazine into the ghost. "You're stressed? Really? Do you want to take a look at my car and tell me what you're stressed about? Because I have to either make up a believable story for the insurance company or pay for that out of pocket."

Helena had the good sense to look a tiny bit contrite. "I'm just saying...oh, never mind." She stalked past Jadyn and passed through the back door of the car into the backseat.

Mildred sighed. "*Now* she's transparent."

CHAPTER SIX

IT TOOK MORE patience than God dispersed for Jadyn to listen to Helena whine all the way home about her sore hip and lost pie. The fact that she'd stolen the pie in the first place was completely lost on her and the damage she'd done to Mildred's car had apparently fled her mind. To keep from launching over the seat, Mildred alternated between clenching the seat belt and rolling down the window to stick her head outside. Several times, Jadyn had started to pull over and order the ghost out of the car, but ultimately, it seemed more expedient to just get them all back to the hotel and into separate spaces.

Shortly into the ride back to the hotel, Jadyn tuned out Helena and tried to work what they'd learned at the diner into a logical scenario. Based on what Dee said, Raissa and Zach had been in good spirits while in the diner, and no one sketchy had been present. The bikers had indicated a flat tire where Luc had found Zach.

What made the most sense was that someone came upon them while Zach was changing the tire and stole the car. What didn't make sense is why they took Raissa with them. If they'd only wanted to rob them and steal the car, they would have left them behind...or shot them on the spot, but that was a scenario Jadyn thanked God she didn't have to dwell on.

Unfortunately, the reasons for taking Raissa were all things she needed to dwell on, and Jadyn couldn't think of a single one that led to a tolerable outcome, much less a pleasant one. Statistics said if Raissa wasn't already dead, she would be soon. And if it was a ransom heist, surely they would have been contacted already.

When they finally got back to the hotel, Helena disappeared upstairs, claiming she needed a long, hot bath while Mildred and Jadyn called Maryse and filled her in on what they'd found. Then Jadyn had poured Mildred a shot of whiskey and she'd trudged upstairs to get some rest.

Back in her room, Jadyn paced, too wound up to sit still, much less sleep. She glanced at the clock again and sighed when she saw that only five minutes had passed. The overwhelming feeling that she should be doing something nagged at her. But what? She and Colt would head into the swamps tomorrow morning and the diner end of things had been covered, so what else was there to do?

Knowing she wouldn't be able to sleep until she calmed down, she grabbed her room key and some money and headed across the street to Bill's Bar. Maybe Bill would have some local gossip for her. Granted, Bill's information usually consisted of speculation and exaggeration, but sometimes those things put you onto a new investigative track.

The bar was crowded for a weeknight, and Jadyn wondered how many were here to whisper their theories about Raissa and Zach. She made her way over to the bar and gave Bill a wave. He headed straight for her and before she could even ask, poured her a beer.

"On the house," he said.

"Thanks," she said. "It's been a long day."

He nodded. "Everyone's been talking about it. Kinda hushed, if you know what I mean, but I hear most of what's said."

"What are people saying?"

"Everything from criminals they arrested got them to they were attacked by the Honey Island Swamp Monster."

"Is he stealing cars now?"

Bill smiled. "In the bayou, everything is possible." He glanced around, then leaned across the bar. "Some of the guys overheard those FBI agents talking in front of the hotel, and they said Zach emptied his weapon at the scene. You don't have to tell me nothing that will get you into trouble..."

"It's true."

Bill frowned. "I was hoping they'd misunderstood."

"Yeah. It does make things appear more dire."

"It's not just that." He glanced around the bar again and frowned. "Some people are saying Raissa and Zach were dirty and whoever they were fronting for called his mark. Now, I am the first to say that's total bullshit, but in these small towns where not much goes on, people sometimes flap their mouths a bit much."

"Any reason why people would want to make up tales about Raissa and Zach?"

He shrugged. "Jealousy, boredom, too much HBO, just plain crazy. Take your pick. That last little bit of criminal activity you were involved in didn't do much to curb people's imagination. They're dreaming up everything from the Mafia to international drug lords living in Mudbug."

She nodded. "I'm sure it's nothing. I can't imagine Colt, Luc, Maryse, Mildred, and a host of others being friends with Zach and Raissa and having no idea they were on the take."

"Exactly. I haven't heard anything of real merit so far, but I'll keep my ear to the bar and if I do, you'll be the first to know."

"Thanks, Bill."

The door opened and Bill glanced over then looked back at Jadyn and grinned. "Your boyfriend's here."

Jadyn didn't know why she expected to see Colt standing there, but she was wrong. Bart and his friend Tyler, a pair she'd met her first day on the job, strolled in. Bart scanned the bar and when he locked onto her, he headed straight for the empty stool to her left. Bill gave her a wink and reached for two beer mugs.

Jadyn shuffled uncomfortably on her stool. Bart had made his interest in her clear, and while he seemed like a nice guy and he definitely wasn't hard on the eyes, for some reason, he hadn't caught her attention.

You know the reason.

She held in a sigh and smiled at Bart, determined to put the aloof Colt Bertrand out of her mind.

"Hi," Bart said and gave her a big smile. "How's it going?"

"Tough day," she said.

He sobered and nodded. "We heard about Zach and Raissa. That's bad news. How is Mildred holding up?"

Her heart warmed a bit that he'd thought to ask about Mildred, and she chided herself for not giving Bart a chance. What's the worst that could happen—she'd end up with a friend who was a guy? Life definitely held worse things.

"She's doing okay, considering. Just feeling kinda helpless, like the rest of us."

"Does the FBI have any idea what happened?" Bart asked.

Tyler snorted. "Like they'd tell anybody if they did."

"Unfortunately," Jadyn said, "Tyler's right. If they have any thoughts on what happened and why, they're not sharing them."

"I guess they haven't found the car, either?" Bart asked.

"Not that I've heard," Jadyn said. She and Colt had already agreed to keep their dive discovery a secret. Once the FBI pulled the car out of the pond tomorrow, word would get around.

"That Caddy is older but it's a sweet ride. It doesn't surprise me that someone would want it."

Bart looked over at his friend. "Really? You think someone stole the car and decided to take Raissa with them? What are you, stupid?"

Tyler's jaw flexed and Jadyn could tell he wasn't happy about being called stupid. "Maybe she ran off into the swamp when the shooting started, fell and hit her head or something. She wouldn't be the first person lost in these swamps."

"That's true enough, but the FBI had their dogs out today," Jadyn said. "They didn't catch any scent of her. If she's in the swamps, the entry point wasn't where Zach was found."

"Is Colt working the case?" Bart asked.

"No. It's not his jurisdiction. The FBI is running the investigation."

"That figures" Tyler interjected. "I bet the FBI think they're too smart to get help from one of us small-town Joes."

Bart shook his head. "If that's the case, they're stupid. I'm sure there's plenty of people who's got away with stuff the FBI never even caught wind of."

"My guess is, you're both right," she said.

Tyler downed the rest of his beer and tossed some bills on the counter.

"You leaving already?" Bart asked.

"Some of us gotta work for a living."

"I work," Bart argued.

"Three days a week ain't working," Tyler said as he walked away. "That's vacationing."

Jadyn checked her watch and held in a yawn. Finally, the day had caught up with her. "I should get out of here, too. I've got to get an early start tomorrow."

Bart didn't bother to hide his disappointment. "You sure you can't stay a bit longer?"

"I wish I could, but I'm beat and I have to get up early."

"Then I guess I'll have to take you to dinner to give you my undivided attention."

She slid off her stool, trying to think of something diplomatic to say. Having a beer by chance in the bar was one thing, but dinner sounded way too much like a date with the underlying possibility of romance. Jadyn wasn't sure she was ready to field that option.

You'd say yes if it were Colt.

"I'll give that some thought," she said, determined to break the frustrating cycle of being attracted to a man who'd made it clear he wasn't interested in anything but a working relationship.

"Don't think too hard or you'll say no," he said and winked.

She laughed, her discomfort easing. Maybe she should have dinner with Bart. A man who could make you laugh definitely had a lot of value.

"I won't," she said. "Have a good night."

"You too."

As she walked back to the hotel, she promised herself she'd give Bart's dinner offer serious thought. She'd already given Colt plenty of time to make a move, and he'd chosen instead to distance himself. It was time to let thoughts of Colt Bertrand go.

———

BEFORE DAWN, Jadyn crept downstairs, hoping to put on a pot of coffee without disturbing any patrons or Mildred. She'd fallen asleep quickly, but her sleep hadn't been restful. Instead, she'd tossed and turned, her mind racing with frantic dreams that disappeared from her memory the instant she awakened.

She knew the dreams came from the pressure she felt to find Raissa. The dreams had always come when something weighed heavily on her. And this was the worst situation she could recall being in. She and Colt had to make progress today. Time was running out.

If it hadn't already.

She shook her head as she walked down the hallway to the downstairs kitchen. A clear head was important for today's work. Getting more stressed or even depressed would decrease her awareness and she needed to be on top of her game. As she pushed open the kitchen door, Jadyn was surprised to see Mildred already inside, pouring a cup of coffee.

"What are you doing up so early?" Jadyn asked. "I didn't disturb you moving around, did I?"

Mildred waved a hand and poured a cup of coffee for Jadyn. "I was disturbed all right, but it had nothing to do with you. I had these horrible nightmares about being chased by large killer clowns wearing spandex. They were throwing apple pies at me."

Jadyn grinned. "Given the source of the nightmares, I know I shouldn't find it funny, but I have to admit that it's got a certain level of humor to it."

Mildred slid into a chair at the tiny breakfast table and dumped what looked to be a half a cup of sugar into her coffee. "If it had happened to anyone else, I would probably find it funny too. Truth be told, once I get done being pissed over the car repair, I'll probably find it funny. But I'd never let Helena know that."

"No way," Jadyn agreed as she sat down across from Mildred. "Milk the car situation for as much guilt as you can manage to get out of Helena."

Mildred gave her a rueful look. "It's going to be far less than I'd like. So you and Colt are heading out early?"

Jadyn nodded. "We wanted to get out of sight of the feds before daylight."

"How's Colt going to get around jurisdiction? Didn't Agent Ross tell him to stay out of the swamps? He could probably make trouble for Colt if he wanted to. I'd hate to see him get ousted from his job over this."

"No worries," Jadyn said. "As sheriff, Colt may not have a valid reason to be in the swamps, but I do. As of five o'clock yesterday, Colt is officially on vacation from the sheriff's department. And as of first thing this morning, he is officially a contractor working for the Department of Wildlife and Fisheries."

Mildred smiled. "That is brilliant. Do you think it will hold?"

"Even if the FBI pushes Wildlife and Fisheries to change their mind, it will take days or a week to get anything through that quagmire. At the very least, we'll have time to inspect all the camps."

"That's my girl. Beautiful and smart."

Jadyn felt a blush creep up her neck. She wasn't used to being complimented, especially by matronly women. Her own mother had been less than complimentary about, well, mostly everything that had to do with Jadyn.

"It was actually Colt's idea," she said.

"Fair enough," Mildred said, "but he's not as pretty as you."

Jadyn laughed. "He's probably okay with that."

A buzzer rang at the front door of the hotel and Jadyn glanced at her watch. "Colt's not due for another thirty minutes," she said as she jumped up and headed down the hall for the lobby.

She could see the silhouette of a person outside the frosted glass of the front door, but the figure didn't look tall enough to be Colt. She checked for her weapon, then unlocked the door and opened it a bit.

Maryse peered through the crack at her. "Stop staring and let me in," she said. "I haven't had coffee yet."

Jadyn opened the door for Maryse to enter and she headed straight down the hall to the kitchen without another word. Jadyn hurried behind her, wondering what had caused her normally upbeat and late-sleeping cousin to take on sullen and early riser.

She entered the kitchen a few steps behind Maryse, who went straight for the coffeepot. Jadyn looked over at Mildred, who raised one eyebrow. Jadyn shrugged and slipped back into her chair. Whatever had caused Maryse's personality shift was bound to come out sooner or later. So far, Jadyn hadn't seen any indication that her cousin was a closet brooder.

Maryse sat her coffee down so hard on the table that it sloshed over the side. She cursed and grabbed a handful of napkins, stuffing them all under the cup before dumping even more sugar than Mildred had used in her cup. Jadyn briefly wondered if it wouldn't be healthier to forgo the sugar and just add a shot of whiskey.

"So," Mildred asked, "what brings you out this early?"

"Don't want to talk about it," Maryse grumbled and set to stirring her coffee with the force of a Category 5 hurricane.

Jadyn looked at Mildred, hoping to take a cue from the hotel owner, but she was staring at Maryse, looking as perplexed as Jadyn felt. Okay, so whatever was up with her cousin was so far outside of the norm that even Mildred didn't have a guess.

Finally, Maryse stopped stirring and looked at Jadyn. "You going to tell the feds about what that biker said?"

"Not right away. I'm going to talk it over with Colt first and see what he thinks. All that information does is answer the question of why that particular location and why Zach was out of the car. It doesn't help at all with finding Raissa."

Mildred nodded. "And if the feds find out we were at the diner asking questions, they'll bring a rash of crap down on Jadyn. Ross is just looking for a reason to get Wildlife and Fisheries to bench her."

"Ross is a douche bag," Maryse said. "Most feds are."

Because her cousin was married to a federal agent, Jadyn wisely decided to remain quiet. Luc hadn't seemed remotely douche-baggy to her, but perhaps Maryse's comment was an indication of why her mood was so foul. Marital discord couldn't possibly be fun.

"Is Colt picking you up here?" Maryse asked.

"Yes. He should be here any minute."

"You taking Helena?"

"God no! Last time she was supposed to be shadowing me, she couldn't keep up with a walk down the street. Can you imagine her keeping up with Colt and me getting in and out of the boat and tromping through the swamp? Not like I can tell Colt to wait for her to catch up."

"You'd end up leaving her somewhere in the swamp," Mildred said, "and then we'd have to hear about it for the next hundred years."

"I'm going with you," Maryse said suddenly.

"Oh." Jadyn looked over at Mildred who shook her head. "I thought Luc wanted you to stay out of the swamp."

A flush started on Maryse's neck and crept up her face. "I don't give a damn what he wants. This is an emergency."

"An emergency that Jadyn and Colt can handle," Mildred pointed out.

Maryse shook her head, her expression leaving no doubt that she'd dug in her heels. "They can't cover all the camps in one day. If I cover part, we can get them all done."

"Luc wouldn't ask you to stay away from the swamps unless it was critical," Mildred argued. "It's too dangerous."

"I've got my gun," Maryse said.

Jadyn rubbed her hand across her mouth. The last time her cousin had brandished a weapon, it hadn't turned out so good for a hutch, an urn, and her dead father's ashes.

"Ahhh," Mildred said, "you're not exactly a sharpshooter. If you got into trouble, I don't know that you'd be able to handle it."

"So I'll take Jadyn with me. She's a crack shot and Colt doesn't need any help."

Jadyn froze. She'd connected with her cousin from the first moment they'd met, and she definitely cared a lot about her, but no way did she want to be in a boat all day with a pissed-off, gun-toting Maryse. Frantically, she ran through a list of reasons they couldn't ride out together.

"I have to go out with Colt," Jadyn said, latching onto the one logical reason she could come up with. "Technically, he's my contractor, which is why he has the right to be in the swamps. If Agent Ross or his men catch him out there alone, they'll arrest first and ask questions later. If I'm there, it will get him a pass, at least for a while."

Maryse slumped down in her chair and crossed her arms across her chest. "Then I'll go with you two and it will take twice as long to get the job done, but I'm not sitting in my office all day pretending nothing is wrong."

A knock at the kitchen door broke into Jadyn's thoughts and she whirled around to see Colt standing in the doorway. They'd been so busy arguing, she hadn't even heard him come in.

"Am I interrupting?" Colt asked.

"Yes," Maryse said, "but that's never stopped anybody in this town before. You may as well come in."

After a moment of hesitation, he stepped inside.

"Look," Jadyn said to Maryse, "I understand how you feel, and in your shoes, I'd feel the same way. But it's a really bad idea."

Maryse sat up straight in her chair, her expression moving from sullen to angry. "You think I'm going to let some...some *man* tell me what to do?"

"He's not some man," Mildred said. "He's your husband."

Colt shifted uncomfortably. "Maybe I should wait outside."

"No!" Maryse said. "You're part of this."

Colt's eyes widened. "Me?"

Maryse nodded. "I want to go with you and Jadyn today to

search the camps. I probably know this swamp better than anyone."

"Probably." Colt looked over at Jadyn and Mildred. "I get the feeling I missed an important part of this conversation."

Mildred shot a frustrated look at Maryse. "You missed the part where Luc said he doesn't want her in the swamp because of a case he's working."

"Oh." Colt shoved his hands in his pocket, looking more uncomfortable than Jadyn had ever seen him. "That puts a different spin on things. If Luc says no, then it's no."

Maryse narrowed her eyes at him. "I thought you had a pair."

"Did when I dressed this morning," he said, "and even though you like to walk down streets in a robe and carrying a handgun, I'm more afraid of what Luc would do to me if I let you go with us."

"Coward," Maryse said.

"Yes, ma'am."

Jadyn held in a smile, mentally giving Colt points for both intelligence and knowing how to win an argument with a woman.

"You ready?" Jadyn asked Colt, hoping to get out of the hotel before Maryse launched another offensive.

"Hell, yeah."

Jadyn rose from her chair and gave her cousin's arm a squeeze. "Please don't be mad. I haven't known Luc very long but he doesn't strike me as the type of guy who'd ask you to do something like this unless it was really important."

Maryse glared at her for a couple of seconds, then sighed. "You think I don't know that? But this is Raissa we're talking about."

Her voice broke as she delivered the last sentence, and Jadyn's heart broke a little. She knew that helpless feeling all too well, and wished more than anything that she could alleviate her cousin's pain. But right now, she couldn't think of a single way to help besides finding Raissa and returning her to the people who loved her.

"Colt and I are going to find her," Jadyn said, even though she knew it was a promise she might not be able to keep.

"You do that, and you bring her home safe to Zach."

Jadyn gave her a nod and followed Colt out of the hotel.

"Long morning?" he asked as they climbed into his truck.

"You have no idea."

"Normally, I wouldn't ask about women's business, but what's up with Maryse and Luc?"

She shook her head. "I don't know exactly. He's being really secretive about the whole thing—has been for a couple of weeks now, according to Maryse. I know he can't talk about his cases, but I wish he'd tell her more than just 'don't go into the swamps unless absolutely necessary.'"

He frowned. "I've known Luc for years. Worked with him on a couple of cross-agency cases when I was with the New Orleans police. I know Maryse is his wife and that makes things different, but he's never been an alarmist. Maryse doesn't have any idea what kind of case he's working?"

"No, and it's not from lack of asking." Jadyn looked over at him. "You don't think it has anything to do with Raissa and Zach, do you?"

He shook his head. "I don't see how, and case or no, Luc would have said something to me if he thought there was cross-over. I'm positive he would have told me to be on the lookout if something he was working on was happening in Mudbug, especially given that his family and friends live here."

Jadyn looked out the window as they drove up to the dock. "So it sounds like Luc is specifically worried that someone will come after Maryse because of him?"

"That's what it sounds like to me."

"And with Raissa missing, he can't help but think it has something to do with her and Zach's work. So now, he's probably doubly stressed. His worst nightmare is staring him directly in the face."

Colt nodded. "I'm sure it's crossed his mind more than once."

"That's got to suck."

"Especially when you're married to a woman like Maryse. She probably hasn't given him a moment of peace since the first edict."

"I'm sure she hasn't."

"You know, based on everything we learned yesterday, I'm leaning toward Raissa's disappearance being unrelated to her being an FBI agent. I was going to give Luc a call last night and bring him up to date, but I got sidetracked with a local crime spree and forgot."

"Crime spree?"

"Yes, one of Old Man Humphrey's many nonworking vehicles disappeared from his front lawn."

"You think someone stole it? Doesn't sound like the type of car people are clamoring to own."

"Something big is gone from that spot in the yard. The problem is Humphrey's ninety years old if he's a day and likes his whiskey. For all I know, he could have sold it and forgotten or even driven the darn thing off himself."

Jadyn smiled. "Sounds like a real mystery."

"Yeah, but I'll take drunken seniors with questionable missing cars over this mess with Zach and Raissa any day."

"I bet," Jadyn said, trying to figure out a way to tell Colt that she and Mildred had visited the diner the night before. It had been Colt's idea to question the diner employees, and she wasn't sure how he'd take her and Mildred beating him to the punch.

Finally, she decided to simply blurt it out. "I had a night adventure myself. Mildred and I went to that diner up the highway. I knew we'd be in the swamp all day today and a good part of tomorrow, and Mildred was itching to do something…"

"Makes sense that she would be," he said, not sounding remotely irritated at their action.

"We played it off as the worried aunt and cousin, figuring the family angle would get us more."

Colt nodded. "That's smart. Did it work?"

"Yes and no. I mean, we got information, but nothing that helps us find Raissa." She relayed the conversations with Dee and the biker to Colt.

He started frowning as soon as she got to what the biker said, probably running through the list of scenarios just like she had.

"Sounds like a crime of opportunity," he said.

"Yeah, that's what I think, too, but why take Raissa? I don't like it."

"Neither do I," he said as he pulled up to the dock. "Hopefully, we can find something today. The longer this goes…"

Jadyn nodded as she grabbed her backpack from the backseat of the truck. He didn't have to say it out loud. She'd already processed every horrible possibility.

CHAPTER SEVEN

MARYSE STOMPED across the hotel lobby for the hundredth time that morning and flopped onto the lobby couch. "What good is a day off if you're held hostage?"

Mildred looked over the counter, one eyebrow raised. "Don't see any handcuffs from where I sit, but if you keep throwing yourself onto my lobby furniture, I might find a pair."

"If you're looking for something to do," Helena said, "one of the cooks at the diner pulled a blackberry cobbler out of the oven about ten minutes ago. I wouldn't mind eating a blackberry cobbler."

"You mean a slice of cobbler?" Mildred asked.

"No, I meant the whole thing, but you and Maryse are welcome to a slice...a small one. That is if Maryse will go buy the cobbler."

"I'm not buying you a cobbler," Maryse said. "After what you made me do to my daddy's urn, I'd see you starve to death first...or whatever happens when you're already dead and starving."

Helena threw her hands in the air. "How many times do I have to apologize for that? Hardly anyone can see me, so I didn't think about how the outfit would look to you. And I'd forgotten that you're not a very good shot."

"I don't know what you're talking about. If you'd been a real person, those bullets would have hit you center mass."

Helena stuck her lower lip out. "I *am* a real person."

"A real *live* person."

"Well, you don't have to be rude about it."

"That's a matter of opinion."

Helena glared. "If that's how you're going to be, I'll just head upstairs and see if that FBI agent who stayed behind is talking to anyone on the phone." A couple seconds later, she stomped up the stairs.

Mildred shook her head. "It's like having two five-year-olds. If you two are going to snipe at each other all day, can you at least take it to the kitchen, or even better, I'll give you my biggest suite. You can bitch 'til the cows come home and it will be out of my earshot."

Maryse gave Mildred an apologetic look. "I'm sorry. I'm not trying to drive you crazy."

"I know you're not, but you're managing to do a good job of it anyway."

"I just hate sitting here. What's so wrong with riding in a boat with Jadyn and Colt? Both of them are great shots."

"Yes," Mildred agreed, "but did you ever stop to think that if Luc is worried about you, then going into the bayou means you might bring trouble with you? That might put Jadyn and Colt in a position they would never be in without you along. They're already facing the possibility of running up on the kidnappers. Do you really want to add another element of danger to that mix?"

Maryse crossed her arms across her chest and frowned. She knew Mildred was right. Had already thought of that herself, although she would have never admitted it. But that didn't mean she had to like it, and by God, she didn't.

"I offered to go by myself," Maryse said. "Remember?"

"Yes, you did. And I'm not saying you should have done it, but if that's *really* what you wanted, you should have just headed out in your boat and sent someone a text message that you were going. The way you did it put Jadyn and Colt in the position of getting between you and Luc. No one in their right mind is going to get in the middle of a marital fray."

Maryse sighed. "You're right. I know you're right—"

"Wheeeeeeee!"

Helena squealed and Maryse looked over to see her sliding down the stair rail. She cringed as the large mass reached the bottom post, but Helena turned transparent and shot off the end. Unfortunately, her transparency didn't last long enough to land.

She hit the floor with a bang and rolled backward into the wall, shaking it to the foundations. A picture hanging above her rattled off and crashed onto the top of her head, splintering the picture from the frame.

Mildred stood up, hands on her hips, and glared at Helena. "What if someone had been at the front desk when you pulled that stunt?"

"But no one's here."

"Did you check to make sure no one was here before you relived your childhood?"

Helena looked guilty.

"I didn't think so," Mildred said. "The last thing I need is a reputation as a haunted hotel."

"But you *are* a haunted hotel," Helena pointed out as she brushed glass off her jeans.

"That's beside the point. People around here are superstitious. If word gets out I have a ghost, business would go to hell in a handbasket. Then you would have nowhere to live and I would have no money to feed you."

Helena frowned. "I guess I didn't think that one through."

"Shocking," Maryse said. "Did you get anything from that stiff upstairs?"

Helena climbed up from the floor and flopped into one of the lobby chairs, breathing as if she'd just run a marathon. "Yeah. He even had the phone on speaker, so I could hear that butthead Agent Ross, too."

"So what's going on?"

Helena grinned. "Well, the funny part is that Agent Stiff was left behind because he's supposed to follow Jadyn when she leaves the hotel."

"He's about two hours late for that one," Mildred said.

Helena nodded. "The idiot even called her lazy because he thinks she's still asleep."

"Ha!" Maryse laughed. "I can't wait to tell her that. Did he say anything else?"

"Yeah, Agent Butthead Ross said they were about to pull the car out of the pond. He's going to have it transported to the garage here in Mudbug, and he's going to do an inspection himself to make sure the car belongs to Raissa. If the car is Raissa's, then he'll call the forensics team who will process the car, looking for evidence related to Raissa and Zach's cases."

Maryse frowned. "I thought Ross told Colt that the FBI didn't think their work had anything to do with this."

Helena rolled her eyes. "And you believe the feds are telling the truth?"

"I have to agree," Mildred said. "No offense to Luc, of course. But the FBI is not going to give up anything they consider confidential. Not even to family, much less friends, and certainly not to what they'd consider competing law enforcement."

"That's crap," Maryse said. "By not telling us everything, they limit our ability to help."

"I think that's the point," Mildred said.

Maryse stared at the painting of the bayou that hung over

the lobby fireplace. "I wish we could find out what they're looking for in that car." She looked over at Helena. "I don't suppose—"

"No way," Helena interrupted. "That's at least fifteen miles' walk from here. By the time I got there, Ross would be retired."

"Who said you had to walk?"

"I took that part for granted. Mildred won't have any part of it because she's too smart to go there, you're grounded, and I can't exactly drive there myself. Well, I could, but that might cause some concern."

Maryse jumped off the couch. "I'm not grounded."

Mildred shook her head. "No way. There's only one road that leads to that pond and it's a dead end. You have nowhere to go if the FBI catches sight of you."

"There's a path about a mile from the end. I can pull off on it and hide the truck with some brush in case anyone passes by."

"Oh no," Helena said. "I'm not walking a mile unless there's blackberry cobbler in it for me."

"You get me something that helps this investigation," Maryse said, "and I'll buy you a slice."

"Three."

"Two."

"Done. Whoohoo! Blackberry cobbler."

Mildred gave them both a look of dismay. "I don't know which one of you is worse."

Instantly, Maryse sobered. "You're not going to tell Luc, are you?"

"Not unless he asks me directly. I'm not about to voluntarily unleash that can of worms."

"Thank God," Maryse muttered.

"But I won't lie for you, either. So you either get in and out without incident, or you better get a speech prepared."

"Don't worry," Maryse said. "We will be incident-free."

Mildred raised her eyebrows, clearly not convinced that anything involving Helena could be incident-free.

For that matter, neither was she.

———

COLT EASED the game warden boat around a sharp left turn in the bayou, scanning ahead for other boats, particularly any occupied by Ross and company. He would have preferred to take his own boat, but Jadyn had pointed out that using her equipment made the contractor thing look more legitimate. She had a pad of paper with drawings of different sections of the swamps that she'd been reworking. The cover story was that Colt was helping her remap the area since Jadyn didn't know it well and the existing set of maps hadn't been updated since the last hurricane, which had shifted things significantly.

The channel they traveled was about half a mile from Boudreaux's Pond, where Colt hoped Ross would remain stationed with his team rather than wandering around the area. It made logical sense to check the camps surrounding the pond first. And technically, everything was official with the contractor job, but Colt knew they'd catch hell if Ross caught them nearby.

As he directed the boat toward the middle of the bayou, he was pleased to see a clear stretch about a mile long. The occasional fisherman was probably tucked away out of sight under the cypress trees that hung over the water, but he couldn't think of a single reason Ross would be lurking under a canopy of tree limbs. If he was on the channels, he'd most likely be in the middle, in plain sight, which meant that so far, they were in the clear.

"Maryse said we couldn't cover all the camps in one day," Jadyn said as Colt directed the boat toward a dilapidated dock.

"She's right. We'll need another half day to cover them all. But

I'm hoping we find something today and seeing the rest isn't necessary."

Jadyn nodded. "I hope so too. Who's camp is this?"

Colt grimaced. "Old Man Humphrey's. Can't you tell by the ten nonworking refrigerators scattered in the weeds in front of it? He must have settled for appliances since he couldn't get automobiles down here."

Jadyn smiled. "One day, when things are right again, I'm going to drive out to Old Man Humphrey's house just to see what all the complaining is about. And if I feel like being insulted a bit, I might even knock on the door and strike up a conversation."

"You've got to really be lacking in company to seek out Humphrey." He drew the boat up to the dock and Jadyn reached for a post.

"It's not that," she said as she tied off the post. "I just figure I can do my job better if I know what I'm working with. I've met a lot of people since I've been here, but some of the old-timers are almost hermits. I figure I'm going to have to go to them for any exposure."

"Exposure is a good choice of word. God only knows what you may get spending time with the recluses I can think of. And you definitely want to announce yourself from the property line. Most of them think shooting first and asking later is their constitutional right."

"Maybe I need to talk to you about getting a bulletproof vest," she said as she stepped onto the wobbly dock.

"It's probably not the worst idea."

"It doesn't look like anyone has been here recently," she said as they pushed their way through the overgrown brush toward the camp.

"No, at least not from this direction."

"Is there a road running behind it?"

"Yeah, about half a mile away from this camp. The gap gets a little wider the farther down the bayou you go."

"A half mile is definitely doable, even with a hostage."

"Ten miles is doable with a hostage as long as you've got a gun on them and there's no witnesses around."

Jadyn sighed. "You know, normally I am the most based-in-reality person I know, but just this once, I wish I could have that 'glass half-full' mentality."

Colt nodded. He understood exactly what Jadyn was saying, but he also knew it was useless to wish for things that could never happen. Some people liked to think that law enforcement work made people—from the positive person's point of view—jaded. But he knew better. If he and Jadyn hadn't already been grounded in reality, neither of them would have been drawn to the work in the first place. Statistics didn't lie. There was always a chance a bad situation could turn out fine, but in law enforcement, you had to be geared to accept that it often didn't.

Keeping that fact in the forefront of your mind minimized disappointment.

Colt walked up the steep steps leading to the camp, trying not to dwell on the disappointment he was going to feel if this case turned out badly. He already knew quite well the odds against a happily ever after, but when it was personal, you tended to push those odds back in place of hope.

He twisted the front doorknob and the door creaked open.

"It's not locked?" Jadyn asked.

"No. A lot of locals don't bother," he said as he stepped inside. "There's not much traffic this deep in the bayou. Visitors tend to fish in the ponds closer to town. Sometimes kids go into camps and have parties, but they won't haul a truckload of beer through the swamp on foot for a half mile when other camps are closer to the roads."

She followed him inside and glanced around. "Not much to see."

"No. A lot of these places are one big room and a bathroom. They're not meant for full-time living. But that makes them easier for us to search."

He crossed the tiny structure and opened a door on the far wall. "Looks like no one's been here for a while."

"Then on to number two," she said, clearly trying to force optimism she didn't feel. "Do you mind giving me a rundown on the owners as we cover the cabins? If it's not a bother?"

"It's no bother," he said as they left the camp and headed back to the dock. "The better you can do your job, the easier it makes mine."

"Great." She released the boat from the dock.

"The next camp is owned by Roscoe Bartlett. He owns the general store. It's been a while since I've been inside, but if I remember correctly, his is nicer than most of the others. Has a separate bedroom and the finish out is more like a house."

Roscoe's camp was indeed nicer than Old Man Humphrey's, at least on the outside. The front of the camp possessed no collection of broken appliances and didn't show any signs of recent passage, until they got to the steps. Two sets of prints showed in the thick layer of dust and led up the steps to the door.

Colt pulled out his nine millimeter and motioned to Jadyn to do the same. "I'll go up first," he whispered. "Wait until I'm on the porch before following. I want to minimize creaking as much as possible."

She gave him a silent nod, and he started up the steps, slowly shifting his weight onto each step. When he stepped onto the porch, he motioned to Jadyn, then pressed his ear to the door. At first, he heard nothing, then he heard a low moan. He checked behind him as Jadyn stepped onto the porch.

"I heard someone inside," he whispers. "Sounds like they're hurt."

He gently turned the knob and was surprised to find it unlocked. He eased the door open and inched his head through the crack until he could see the front room.

It was empty.

On the back wall were two more doors. He crept toward the door on the left, which he thought was the bedroom. As he drew up right in front of the door, a woman screamed.

Immediately, he threw open the door and launched inside, pistol ready for firing. "Stop or I'll shoot!"

The scene inside stopped him so short that Jadyn bumped into him before moving to the side to see what the holdup was. She probably regretted looking.

The screaming woman was clad in hooker-red lingerie and was handcuffed to the posts of the bed, but she wasn't Raissa and the cuffs were plastic. The man in front of her wore black underwear with silver studs and a black mask. He held a leather whip and whirled around to stare at Colt, then froze, the panic clear in his eyes.

Colt grimaced at the sight and shook his head, frowning at both of them. "Sorry to interrupt, Bob. We're looking for a missing person. We'll just get out of here and let you and Jenny get back to...to whatever the hell this is."

He managed to hold in his grin until they left the camp. Jadyn jumped off the steps and hurried up next to him.

"Okay, spill," she said. "Was that Roscoe in the mask? Because you called him Bob. Do you know the woman?"

"No, that definitely wasn't Roscoe, and he'd probably have apoplexy if he knew what was going on in his camp. Despite the mask, I know exactly who the man was—Bob Brant, our illustrious mayor."

Jadyn sucked in a breath. "You're kidding! I've only met him once and he totally gave me the creeps, which makes a lot of sense now. But isn't he married to some woman with a drawn face and entirely too big hair?"

"Yes, that woman is not his wife. She's an eighteen-year-old high school student who babysits his ten-year-old twins."

Jadyn stopped in her tracks. "Oh my God."

He turned back to look at her and grinned. "That's one way of putting it."

She caught up to him and jumped into the boat. "I don't get it. The man's cheating on his wife with essentially a child. So you want to tell me why you're so amused?"

"Because last night Deputy Nelson was on a call about drug use behind the school." He started the boat and headed down the bayou. "The supplier was the mayor's seventeen-year-old son, and he would have made my life hell if I pressed charges. But now..."

"He's not going to say a word." Jadyn smiled. "I wonder what his son will think when daddy doesn't bail him out again."

"I'm sure he won't think much of it, and as he'll be sitting in my jail for a bit, I'm also sure I'll get to hear all about it from him any time I'm in earshot. Even more interesting is what the mayor's wife will think about his not saving her baby."

"Sounds like you're looking forward to it."

"That kid has been running wild since junior high school. If he doesn't straighten out soon, best case is he'll be living at home until he's forty. Worse case, he'll live behind bars. Going to jail for a while might be the one thing that could knock some sense into him."

"I've known kids like that, and you're probably right. What about the girl the mayor was with? Where's she headed?"

"Probably to a pole in New Orleans. Everyone in my position has tried with that one, but she's determined to wreck her life. If you knew her parents, you know she comes by it honest. I'll just be glad when she graduates and moves her drama out of Mudbug."

Jadyn shook her head. "I guess small towns are no different than big cities when it comes to the sordid happenings behind closed doors."

"Yeah, only people in small towns work harder to hide things, because once they're out, it doesn't take ten minutes for every resident to know their secrets."

He directed the boat to the next dock, hoping this inspection yielded a more important revelation than the last. And one that didn't have his breakfast repeating.

————

MARYSE BACKED her truck into a clearing off the main path and parked. She waved toward a stack of brush. "Get some of that and put it in front of the truck," she said to Helena.

Helena mumbled under her breath but grabbed a dead bush and hauled it over to cover the bumper. Maryse threw a tarp over the top and hood of the car and placed some branches on top of both. After a dozen trips for more covering, she stepped back and inspected their work.

"I don't think anyone will notice," she said.

Helena looked at the camouflaged car and nodded. "Unless someone is specifically looking for a car, it just looks like another clump of dead brush."

"Great," Maryse said and picked up her backpack from behind the bush where she'd stored it. "We can't risk taking the road, so we'll travel just off of it in the swamp."

"Spider and snakes and prickly trees. I can't wait."

"You're one to bitch," Maryse said. "None of those things can hurt you."

"None of those things are *supposed* to hurt me, but you never know. When I go solid, I sometimes feel whatever happens to me."

"Really?" Maryse had always figured the ghost was playing drama queen but maybe she'd judged her too harshly.

"It's only for a second or two—like a flash of memory that's gone when you blink—but for that second, it hurts just as bad as it would if I were alive."

"Still, a one-second recovery time is not bad."

"I guess not. Hey, are you sure you should be coming with me?"

"Do you know where the pond is?"

"No, but what if you get caught by Agent Friendly?"

"I won't get caught. I'll get you close enough to give you directions, then I'll skirt around the pond and watch from the other side with my binoculars."

"I guess that will work."

"It's going to have to." Maryse trudged down the narrow path, pushing branches to the side, wondering all the while just how many things she didn't know about Helena. Given Helena's propensity for keeping secrets and complete lack of communication skills, she figured a lot.

What the hell—they had a bit of a walk. She might as well try to get some of those secrets out of the ghost.

"So," Maryse said, "do you ever plan on telling the truth about why you're back? I mean, the story about pissing off God is funny and believable, but I have a bit more faith in the patience of your creator than that."

She glanced back at Helena, who frowned.

"How come everyone assumes there's a reason?" Helena asked.

"Because people don't ascend and then appear back on earth, and no way am I buying that you're an angel."

"I could be an angel."

"Angels don't steal food."

"Now you're just being picky."

"And you're avoiding the question. Fess up, Helena. You're

back here for a reason, and it's probably one the rest of us need to know. You don't exactly come with a worry-free warranty."

Helena trudged to a stop. "You really want to know?"

Maryse threw her hands in the air. "Of course I want to know. We *all* want to know."

Helena stared down at the ground for a bit, and Maryse began to wonder if she was stalling while she made something up, but when the ghost looked back up at her, she looked incredibly sad.

"I wasn't ready for heaven. Based on the things I helped with when I came back as a ghost, God gave me a trial run, but he finally admitted he'd taken me up too soon. I'm not ready to let go of this life, and my debt on earth isn't paid. So rather than take a permanent demotion in status, I asked to come back and earn my place."

Maryse stared at her. "There's ranking in heaven?"

Helena nodded. "Not like earth, of course. All of the jobs in heaven are good jobs, but the things I want to do only go to those who helped others on earth."

"What about your estate? You gave almost all of it to charities and other worthy causes."

"That definitely helped, but I didn't have to earn the money myself, and giving it to charities didn't require anything physical of me, short of having the will drafted."

"Ah," Maryse said, starting to understand the angle. "You need to get your hands dirty."

"Exactly. And my last stint in Mudbug wasn't enough to push me over the mark. So I'm back here to earn more points."

"Wait. So does that mean all ghosts are here earning brownie points—like some ghostly job fair?"

"Some are. Others are stuck in limbo because of the way they died. They're not able to cross yet because their mind and heart are clinging too hard to the past."

"Like you did last year."

Helena nodded.

Maryse took a minute to consider everything Helena had told her. "Should I even ask what job you want?"

"You can ask, but that's the one thing I'll never tell you. You'll have to die and ascend to find out."

"Yeah, I'll go ahead and wait on that one a while, if you don't mind."

Maryse started walking again and Helena fell in step behind her. Suddenly, she drew up short and Helena piled into the back of her, almost knocking her over.

"What are you trying to do?" Helena complained. "Get us injured?"

Maryse whirled around and stared at her. "You're not here because we're all going to be in danger again, are you? I need you to tell me the truth on this. First Jadyn was in danger and now Raissa's missing..."

Helena held up her hands. "I swear, I didn't have anything to do with either. And if my being sent here was because of those reasons, no one filled me in."

Maryse narrowed her eyes at the ghost, but Helena appeared to be telling the truth. "Hmmmm. Just because no one told you anything doesn't mean that's not the case."

"I suppose that's true," Helena said, looking slightly miserable.

"Well," Maryse said as she took off again. "Nothing to be done about it now, so we may as well do our best while it plays out."

"I hope our best doesn't include snakes and spiders."

"I'm guessing your best doesn't include stealing food, so a few snakes and spiders might even the score."

Helena huffed. "Rude."

Maryse stopped walking again and scanned the swamp surrounding them. "Okay, here's where we part directions. Follow this path about half a mile. Walk twenty yards or so to the right and you'll be on the road. Stay on it until you get to the pond."

"Walk on the road? What if someone sees me?"

Maryse stared at her for a moment.

"Oh, right, no one else can see me." Helena frowned. "Hey, I could have been walking on the road this entire time."

"Oh, I guess you could have."

Helena glared. "You did that on purpose. Probably hoping that a snake would fall on me or something."

"One can always hope," Maryse said before setting off deeper into the swamp.

She skirted through the swamp some distance from the pond, but because she knew the swamps so well, she knew exactly when to break right and head for the back side. She'd told Helena she was going to watch from the other side, but in thinking it over, decided her view would be too restricted from that distance to get much out of it. But she could watch from where the pond curved around to the left. It would be far enough away that no one should notice her, but close enough that she would be able to see anything worth seeing.

Even at a fast clip, it took her almost twenty minutes to get where she wanted. As she crept toward the tree line, she lowered herself to remain unseen behind the decreasing height of the brush. Finally, she stooped behind a shrub and pulled out her binoculars. Using a couple of sticks, she created a hole in the bush, then lifted the binoculars and focused on the crowd of men standing next to a tow truck about fifty yards from her.

She recognized Agent Ross immediately as he stood in front of the other men, waving his hands and giving out orders. A couple minutes later, the men dispersed, each moving to his assigned task. Ross walked to the edge of the pond with the man wearing scuba gear. The tow truck backed up as far as possible toward the muddy bank and the diver grabbed the tow hook and started walking with it into the pond.

Where the hell was Helena?

The ghost had one-third the walk Maryse had, and should have been in place already. Maryse scanned the entire area, looking for some sign of the ghost. She almost missed her completely before realizing that the black lump on the bank, which she'd originally taken for a bag of gear, was actually Helena, decked out in a scuba suit. For the first time since they'd left the hotel, Maryse was glad she had to keep her distance. The scuba suit looked bad enough from a distance. No way did she want a closer view.

As the diver disappeared below the surface of the pond, Helena popped up, or at least, Maryse assumed she did, as the wetsuit got taller but not much thinner. Then she started walking toward the pond.

"Oh no."

What in the world was Helena thinking? The woman ran screaming bloody murder from harmless spiders, but she was walking into a pond that contained alligators and God only knew what else. And how the hell was Helena supposed to find out what Ross was up to if she was playing Jacques Cousteau?

Aggravated beyond belief, Maryse rose up and crept around the edge of the tree line, closer to where Ross and his men were stationed. If she could just get a little closer, she may be able to read his lips. It was something she'd always been fairly good at but never copped to. It got her a lot of information that other people thought she couldn't overhear.

She was about thirty feet away before she could make out things out clearly.

"Did you talk to Assistant Director Richards?" he asked the other agent.

The agent nodded, but Maryse couldn't tell what the reply was as the agent's back was to her.

"Does he think Agent Bordeaux's disappearance has anything to do with the Riley case?" Ross asked.

The agent shook his head.

"She was carrying her ID. Whoever took her has got to know she's a federal agent."

The other agent shook his head again.

"Let me know as soon as you hear something. I need to get this wrapped up before the local law enforcement messes up my investigation. Speaking of which, I need you to run a check on a couple of locals—"

Ross abruptly stopped talking and looked toward the pond. Maryse panned over with her binoculars, expecting to see the diver emerging from the pond, but it was much, much worse.

A section of the pond was whitecapping, as if something large thrashed about below the surface. A second later, Helena bolted out of the water, screaming like someone was killing her.

"Alligators! They're everywhere." She streaked past Ross, running at breakneck speed.

Directly toward Maryse.

CHAPTER EIGHT

ABOUT HALFWAY TO the tree line where Maryse was hidden, Helena tripped over a rotted tree trunk and went sprawling into a clump of dead brush. The brush broke under her weight and went flying into the air in a hundred different pieces.

Crap. Helena had gone solid.

Maryse prayed that Ross hadn't noticed the exploding brush, but her prayer was a second too late. Ross's head jerked in her direction, and he yelled to the other agent as he started running in her direction, gun drawn.

Do something!

But she couldn't move. If she ran, Ross would fire at her. If she stayed still, maybe he'd stop at the brush and wouldn't see her at all. She dropped down as low as she could get, taking refuge as much as she could behind a cypress tree, and peered around it.

Ross stopped where Helena fell and leaned over to inspect the ground, then straightened and scanned the surrounding area. Helena popped up out of the nearby marsh grass and took off running again. Maryse could see the grass collapsing with her every footstep and knew she was still solid. Unfortunately, Ross saw the footprints as well and headed right after her.

Are you watching, God? Negative ten points, at least!

Helena was about twenty feet away from Maryse's hiding place when she screamed again, and stopped so abruptly that she almost toppled over.

"Snake!" she screamed and spun around, tackling Agent Ross like an NFL linebacker.

Ross discharged his weapon as he fell, causing the other agents to run toward him. Maryse popped up from the ground, ready to sprint for the far reaches of the swamp while everyone was distracted. But as soon as she whirled around, she heard a footstep behind her.

"Where the hell do you think you're going?" a man's voice sounded behind her.

She turned around and found herself looking directly into the barrel of a nine millimeter.

"This way," he said, and waved the gun back toward the pond.

Stupid!

She'd completely forgotten about the other agent. He must have circled around while Ross came straight at her. As she stepped out from behind the tree, she saw Ross showing the diving mask to the other agents and waving his hand toward the pond. She scanned the area, but Helena was nowhere in sight. With the panic she was in, she might have run all the way to Canada.

If only Maryse was that lucky.

As they approached the group of agents, a boat engine roared to life and took off down the bayou like a gunshot. Everyone spun around, including the FBI diver, who was halfway up the bank. Maryse held in a groan. There was no mistaking the very rotund driver, clad in a diver's suit.

Agent Ross spun around and fixed his gaze on her. "Who are you working with?"

"I...I'm not working with anyone."

"You expect me to believe my boat drove off by itself?"

"I don't care what you believe. I'm not here with anyone else."

Not anyone alive, at least.

Ross's face flushed with anger and he lifted the binoculars from her chest. "Someone sent you to spy on me," he said, shaking the binoculars, "and I want to know who."

"No one sent me. No one is working with me. I'm a botanist. All my work is based on the plant life in these swamps."

Ross let go of the binoculars and they thumped against her chest. "Not anymore it's not. I suggest you find a nice rosebush in someone's front lawn to study. No one is allowed to go poking around this area of the swamp until I say so."

Maryse felt the blood rush up her neck and onto her face. His arrogance had finally put her in the red, and although Maryse knew it was probably best to be political about the entire thing, she had never managed polite when she was pissed.

"Nothing you or anyone else can say will keep me out of this swamp."

"Really? If you push the issue, I'll have you arrested for trespassing and interfering in a federal investigation."

She gave him a smug smile. "I own the entire game preserve. Good luck making either of those stick."

"The state owns the game preserve."

She shook her head. "The state leases the game preserve from me, but I own the land and have the legal right to occupy or work on any square inch I see fit. Read the lease documents sometime."

Ross threw his arms in the air. "You can't possibly have purchased an entire swamp."

"No. I inherited it from my former mother-in-law, Helena Henry."

Ross froze, apparently recognizing the name. "Helena Henry?"

Maryse nodded.

Ross cursed under his breath. "You're Luc LeJeune's wife."

"The one and only, and he's going to be thrilled when he hears how you've manhandled me." She lifted the binoculars. "I bruise easily."

Ross's eyes widened and he spun around to yell at one of his men. "Get her to the hospital and make sure she's not injured. Drive slowly and don't let her out of your sight until I get there to question her. No phone calls to her husband, either. If the hospital wants to release her, ask for a psych eval, but whatever you do, don't let her leave before I get there."

"Yes, sir. What's the reason for the arrest?"

"We're the damned FBI. It's none of the hospital's business why we're detaining her. Now someone get me a boat so we can go after her accomplice!"

The agent grabbed Maryse by the arm. "This way."

His grip was tight enough to make her wince and she held in a smile. She hadn't lied about bruising easily. Ross was just digging himself a deeper grave. The agent directed her to a truck and motioned for her to get inside. Then he reached into the glove compartment and brought out a pair of handcuffs.

Maryse stared at him. "Seriously?"

"You're a suspect."

"Suspected of occupying my own property? Technically speaking, you guys are the ones trespassing."

He clicked the handcuffs around her wrists. "You can tell all that to your attorney."

Before she could reply, he slammed the door. She watched as he walked around the vehicle, unable to believe how ridiculous the entire situation had become. Looking in the side mirror, she could see Ross, directing the extraction of the car from the pond. Farther up the bayou, a boat approached. Apparently, Ross's backup had arrived.

The arresting agent climbed into the driver's seat and pulled away from the pond. Only then did the entirety of her situation hit Maryse, and a sliver of panic ran through her. Not because she had been arrested—she knew good and well they couldn't make anything stick—and facing a judge didn't worry her in the least.

Facing her husband was an entirely different story.

———

JADYN CLIMBED BACK in the boat, mentally calculating how many cabins they'd covered, then checked her watch. "That makes twenty so far."

Colt nodded and directed the boat down the bayou. "And we haven't found a single thing. I'm beginning to wonder if we're going about this all wrong."

"What do you mean?"

"Maybe it was a miscalculation to start near where the car was found. Maybe he dumped the car away from wherever he's hiding to throw us off track."

Jadyn sighed. It made sense...as much as any of this did. "So do we shift focus to the east side of the swamp or finish up here first?"

"I wish I knew."

He looked as defeated as Jadyn felt. With every empty search, her spirits dropped as much as her frustration level rose. With Maryse and Mildred counting on her to deliver results, Jadyn knew the pressure was on, and it was getting to her. What if she failed? What if she found Raissa too late, or God forbid never found her at all?

The grim look Colt wore left her no doubt that he felt the same pressure she did, and probably a whole lot more. He'd known some of these people his entire life. And a crime of this magnitude occurring in his hometown would make him feel even more responsibility to restore things to normal.

On the upside, the pressure and stress of trying to locate

Raissa and the horror of seeing the mayor decked out like an extra in *Pulp Fiction* had completely eliminated any romantic feelings she might have had for Colt.

Until now, when she thought about it.

Crap.

And now that she was thinking about it, despite the perpetual scowl, he still managed to be sexy as hell. No man had a right to look that good when he was feeling that down. It wasn't fair to women. Especially to her.

She sighed. In one flash of thought, she'd undone an entire morning of blockage.

Suddenly, he cut the speed of the boat and she pitched forward a bit. He grabbed his binoculars and focused on a group of trees to their left.

"Shit!" He tossed the binoculars on the bench behind him and made a U-turn before shooting off down another channel.

"What's wrong?"

"It's Ross and he's coming straight for us."

Jadyn's pulse quickened. She had every right to be in the swamp, and Colt's paperwork was all legit, but she'd hoped they wouldn't have to defend that position, especially so soon. "He'll go straight on the main channel, right?"

"That's what I'm hoping."

He whipped the boat around a sharp corner and she clutched her seat to keep her balance. Then the boat hit something and came to a grinding halt. Jadyn launched off her seat and crashed onto the bottom of the boat. Colt jumped around the steering column and knelt beside her.

"Are you okay?"

She sat up and touched her head where she could feel it throbbing. It had a small knot already and she'd bet anything it would be a big one before the day was over. "I'm fine. It's just a bump."

"Let me see." He pushed her hand out of the way and inspected her forehead. "Can you get up?"

She nodded and he extended his hand to help her. A rush of blood ran through her head as she rose, making her slightly dizzy, but a second later, it was gone and all that remained was the dull ache of the bump.

"How do you feel?" he asked. "Are you dizzy?"

"No. My head hurts a little from the bump, but otherwise I'm okay."

"You'll probably be sore as hell tomorrow. I'm sorry about that."

"What happened?"

He shook his head. "I drove right on top of something big, probably a submerged tree. It stopped the boat completely."

"I noticed." She leaned over the side of the boat and peered into the water. "You better take a look at this."

"What?"

"Either I'm having a flashback to yesterday or we're sitting on top of a car."

Colt stepped to the side and peered over. "Unbelievable. It's like..."

His voice trailed off as he scanned the bayou from left to right. Suddenly he hurried to the bow of the boat and looked into the water again, then practically ran to the back of the boat and leaned over so far Jadyn thought he might fall into the water.

"What's wrong?" she asked.

"I think this is Old Man Humphrey's car." He rose back up and faced her. "And I don't think it's the only car down there."

Jadyn stared. "You see other cars?"

"I think so. The water's too murky to be certain."

Jadyn peered over the side of the boat again, trying to see deeper into the muddy water, but she couldn't make out anything past the car hood the boat was lodged on.

"Do you think—oh no!" She pointed down the bayou as the boat they'd seen earlier tore around the corner, sending a giant wake up the bank.

Colt turned to look and cursed. "Don't give him any more than our cover."

Jadyn nodded. She knew how to keep her mouth shut and play a role. It was the only way she'd managed eighteen years in a house with her mother.

Ross dropped his acceleration to nothing about thirty feet in front of them and hurried to the bow of his boat as it coasted to them. When he got close enough, he grabbed the back of their boat to stop his progress, then he stood up and glared.

"I thought I made myself clear," he said. "Neither of you is allowed in the swamp—not in this area."

"And I thought I made myself clear," Jadyn said, "that the swamps are my job, and you have no authority to relieve me of my duties."

Ross's jaw flexed. "Maybe I don't have the authority yet to get you out of my way, but I do have the authority to arrest this man."

Jadyn shook her head. "I'm afraid you're wrong again. You see, Colt is officially on vacation, so he's not here as the sheriff. He's doing some contract work for Wildlife and Fisheries."

She reached into a storage compartment under the steering column and pulled out the paperwork approved by her boss. "Here are the documents. Everything is in order."

Ross snatched the papers from her and scanned them, cursing under his breath the entire time. He shoved them back at her and glared. "This is bullshit. I know what you're trying to pull, and you're not going to get away with it."

Colt raised his eyebrows and pulled three rolled documents from the storage compartment under the backseat. "These are the most recent maps of the area. Everything in red no longer exists. No bullshit. Jadyn is new at the job. She needs help identifying which channels changed after the last hurricane."

"She could have hired someone else. Any fisherman in this town knows the swamps as well as you."

Colt smiled. "Yeah, but I'm prettier to look at."

Ross sputtered for a moment and shifted around, causing his boat to rock. Then he narrowed his eyes and stared down at their boat. "Why isn't your boat rocking?"

"We're lodged on something submerged here. Maybe you could give us a tow off of it."

Ross stared down into the water. "What the hell is that?"

Colt shrugged. "Probably the cabin of a boat. Like I told you yesterday, they're sunk all over this bayou."

Ross looked back up and grinned. "Looks like a real problem. Good luck with it."

He whirled around and stalked back to start up his boat. He threw it in reverse, then tore off down the bayou without so much as a backward glance.

"He's in a hurry," Colt observed.

"Yeah," Jadyn agreed. "Makes you wonder why. He was pissed to find us here, but I got the impression we weren't who he was after."

Colt nodded. "I wonder what's going on."

"No telling. I figure by the time we get back to Mudbug, someone will have an answer."

"I'm sure," Colt said.

"I'm glad you didn't tell him we were lodged on a car."

"He's already got one black car to tow out of these swamps. I don't want to muddy the waters with a second. Besides, Old Man Humphrey's car has nothing to do with Ross or Raissa. No use allowing him to make my job more difficult. I already got to tell Humphrey the car he took Melvina Watkins's virginity in is at the bottom of the bayou."

"Sucks to have your job." Jadyn hoped the game warden position didn't ever involve hearing about people's sexual conquests, especially from a hundred years ago.

"Some days," Colt agreed. "Guess we best get a move on."

He threw one leg over the side of the boat and pushed down. "It's solid as a rock. Can't have been in the water for long."

He swung his other leg over, then pushed the boat off the car. As the bow cleared the last of the top, he jumped inside and knelt down, inspecting the boat bottom. Several seconds later, he cursed.

"Damage?" she asked.

"Yeah. A pretty good tear. It's easily fixed but I don't think we should risk using the boat the rest of the day. We'll have to backtrack to town and pick up my boat."

Jadyn's spirits fell a bit. Backtracking to Mudbug would cost valuable time, and time was already the one thing they didn't have enough of. "Well, if it can't be helped, then it can't. We'll take another look at the maps when we get back to Mudbug—revise our coverage this afternoon if we need to so we can account for the loss of time."

Colt nodded and started up the boat. "I don't think we'll lose more than an hour."

Jadyn took her seat as Colt pushed the boat up the channel as quickly as he dared maneuver in the narrow space. Sixty minutes of lost time probably meant cutting ten camps off their list for the day. Ten more chances to find Raissa was a big loss. Even though Colt was trying to downplay it, she knew he was as frustrated as she was with the setback. But all that frustration had to be pushed down, closed off in the back of their minds so that they were fresh and alert while they were in the swamps.

Distraction caused mistakes. Caused you to overlook things that you might otherwise see. They couldn't afford any mistakes with this. Not a single one.

Colt swung the boat out of the narrow channel and back into the much wider main bayou. As he increased his speed, Jadyn wondered what had caused Ross to rush away from them so quickly. Something was up. Otherwise, she had no doubt he would have stuck around to harass them longer. No, Ross had been after something when he'd come across them, and whatever it was he deemed more important than their trespass against his orders.

As Colt made a hard right turn in the bayou. Jadyn got a full view of Ross's problem.

CHAPTER NINE

THE OTHER BOAT WAS DRIFTING, just off the center of the bayou and so close to the middle that Colt had to break hard to the left to avoid hitting it. He killed the power immediately, and the bow of their boat slammed down on top of the bayou.

Jadyn clutched the seat to avoid being thrown again and looked over at the other boat, holding in a groan. At first glance, it appeared that a person was in the boat, but with a closer look, Jadyn knew Colt was staring at an empty boat.

Helena Henry sat on the middle bench, her hands covering her eyes. As Colt inched Jadyn's boat closer to the other, Helena removed her hands and Jadyn could see that her eyes were red, as if she'd been crying. Helena stared at them, blinking, then finally locked in on Jadyn. She jumped up from the bench, her eyes wide, and waved her hands above her head, as if she needed to flag them down when they were already headed straight toward her.

"Thank God you found me," she said as they drew alongside her boat. "I've been out here for hours. I thought I knew the way back, but I got lost and every time I tried a new direction, I always ended up back here. Now I'm out of gas."

Jadyn glanced over at Colt, who stepped into the other boat, then looked back at Helena and put her finger to her lips. Colt was one of the lucky people who couldn't see or hear Helena, so no way could Jadyn respond. Helena looked over at Colt, then her eyes widened and she nodded. Jadyn rubbed the back of her neck, a million questions hovering at the edge of lips.

Colt reached into the steering column compartment and grabbed some documents from inside. He scanned them quickly, then shoved them back inside.

"This boat belongs to the FBI."

Jadyn cringed. She'd already expected as much, given the source, but it was still slightly startling to have her worst fear confirmed.

"I could have told you that," Helena said.

Jadyn stepped up to the side of the boat and glared at Helena.

Colt scanned the bank in both directions. "I don't know how it got here."

I do.

"Hmmm," Jadyn said, trying not to look at Helena. "Maybe this is what Ross was looking for."

"Maybe, but the tide's coming in. If it was at the pond, it couldn't have drifted here. Someone had to have taken it." He shook his head. "Who the hell would steal a boat from the FBI?"

Jadyn shook her head. "I can't imagine."

Because I don't have to.

"What are we going to do about it?" she asked.

"Nothing," he said. "I figure it's Ross's problem."

"So you're just going to leave it here?"

"Sure. Why not?"

Helena's eyes widened. "Oh hell no! You're not leaving me here. I could starve. I could get eaten by an alligator. Do you know how big the mosquitoes are here at night?"

As Colt stepped back over, Helena dove for their boat. Unfortunately, Colt had pushed the boat away as he stepped inside, and

Helena hit the side with a *thunk*, then dropped like a stone into the bayou, sending a splash of water a good three feet into the air. Jadyn closed her eyes and cringed.

Colt, who'd been about to start the engine, whirled around. "What the hell was that?"

Jadyn peered over the side of the boat as Helena surfaced, sputtering water like a leaky hose. She grabbed the side of the boat and glared at Jadyn.

"Don't just stand there," Helena said. "Get me out of here before something eats me."

Jadyn blew out a breath. How in the world was she supposed to make that work with Colt staring right at her?

"It was something big," she said. "It went under our boat toward the bank."

Colt turned around and leaned over to peer into the water.

As soon as his back was turned, Jadyn reached down and hoisted Helena into the boat, wondering how in the world an incorporeal entity could weigh so much. Helena flopped into the bottom of the boat with a thud. Jadyn cringed, hoping the noise was for her ears only, but no chance.

Colt turned around. "Where did that come from?"

"I think something hit the bottom of the boat," Jadyn said. At least it was the truth. "Maybe we should get back to the dock."

"Probably a good idea," Colt agreed. "I'd hate to get stranded in a leaky boat with something that made that kind of splash lurking around. Whatever it was, it was enormous."

Helena pushed herself upright and glared at Colt. "I am not enormous."

Jadyn coughed, trying to keep from laughing.

"And what do you mean leaky boat?" Helena asked. "What the hell is wrong with you people? Why can't you get equipment that works?"

Jadyn reached into her backpack and pulled out a set of headphones. "My ears are bothering me a bit," she said. "I'm going to put these on, if that's okay."

Colt nodded. "The humidity sometimes bothers people when they're not used to it. Don't let things go until you get an infection."

"Oh no," Helena griped. "You're not going to ignore me. I've got things to tell you—"

Jadyn popped the earphones on as Colt started up the boat. Helena gave her the finger, then crawled onto the front bench and sat in a huff the entire way back to the dock.

When they reached the dock, Colt helped Jadyn get her boat onto the trailer so she could transport it to Marty Breaux's garage and have him patch the tear. Jadyn told him she wanted to check in with Mildred, so he headed to the sheriff's department to get his boat and would be back to pick her up.

As soon as he was out of earshot, Jadyn whirled around. "What the hell is going on? How did you get the FBI's boat?"

"There was an alligator and then a snake and then people starting shooting, so I ran. It was a long walk to Maryse's truck and I didn't have the keys besides, so I jumped in the boat and left."

Jadyn stared. She's known Helena alone in an FBI boat couldn't be a good thing, but this sounded much worse than she'd imagined. "Did Maryse take you to the pond?"

"Yes. We were going to spy on Ross."

"Where is Maryse?"

Helena shrugged. "She was supposed to be watching from across the pond. I guess when all the fray broke out, she high-tailed it out of there."

"What fray?"

"I got solid."

"That doesn't necessarily account for a fray."

Helena looked down at the ground and sighed. "In my haste to get away from the snake, I might have run over Ross, who might have fired his weapon as he fell."

"And then you drove off in his boat. Good God Almighty."

Helena rolled her eyes. "You say that like it's the worst thing you ever heard."

"Hold that thought."

Jadyn pulled out her phone and dialed Mildred. The hotel owner must have had one hand on the phone because she answered before the first ring finished.

"Is Maryse there?" Jadyn asked.

"Nooooo," Mildred said, and Jadyn knew she didn't want to tattle on Maryse.

"I already know she went to spy on Ross."

"Oh no. What happened?"

Jadyn relayed Helena's fun-filled morning.

"What happened to Maryse?" Mildred asked, the panic clear in her voice.

"That's a good question, and one that I and Dastardly the Panicky Ghost can't answer."

"They left here hours ago, and Helena said this happened right after they got there?"

"That's what she says."

"She would have made it back here by now. Even crawling she could have made it back by now. Do you think Ross has her?"

"I don't know," Jadyn replied, but it sounded more and more likely.

"What do I do if Luc comes looking for her? Should I try to find her myself? I've called her cell several times already and it goes straight to voice mail."

Jadyn heard a boat approaching and looked up to see Colt pulling up to the dock. "Colt's back so I have to get off the phone. I'm sending Helena to the hotel. Take her with you and see if you can find Maryse and her truck."

"What if I run into Ross?"

"Tell him the truth—that you know Maryse was working in this area of the swamp this morning but she should have been back by lunch, and you're looking for her because you're worried. I've got to run."

She disconnected and shoved the cell phone back in her jeans pocket. "Get to the hotel," she said to Helena, then turned around and headed down the dock, her creative mind conjuring up all the things that might have happened to Maryse if Ross got his hands on her.

And all the things that might happen to Ross if Luc LeJeune decided his wife had been poorly treated.

The last thought made her smile.

———

MARYSE HAD BEEN HELD captive in a hospital room for going on six hours and every hour seemed longer than the one before. Six straight hours of CNN. No one should endure such torture. Her captor, whom she'd named the Stepford Agent, for his lack of a single original thought, sat in a chair next to the door as if expecting her to make a break for it.

Truth be known, she would have, but every time he'd used the restroom, he'd handcuffed her to the bed, removing the option. When they'd first entered the room, he'd placed her cell phone on a stand in the corner, inches out of reach when she was shackled. She'd tried to snag it with a bedpan the first time he'd taken a potty break, figuring the risk of breaking the screen was worth it as long as she could still make a phone call. If she had to spend another hour closed up in here with Stepford, she might *need* that psych eval.

Unfortunately, she hadn't heard Stepford coming out of the restroom and he'd caught her bedpan-handed. He'd removed her phone from the table and slipped it into his front jeans pocket where she wasn't about to risk going, not even with a bedpan.

"You know it's been hours since I've eaten," she said.

"My orders don't include serving you meals."

"Your orders didn't include peeing either, but I notice you do that when you're so inclined. My digestive system didn't cut off when you kidnapped me. And if something happens to me while you're holding me hostage, you're going to be responsible. Not to mention you're going to look like the biggest dumbass in the world if I have a medical emergency while you're restraining me in a hospital."

Stepford rose from his chair and snapped the cuffs back on her and the bed, glaring the entire time. "I'll get you something from the hospital cafeteria."

"Oh, goody. Gourmet."

"Food is food. Eat it or don't. All I have to do is provide it."

"Whatever. If they have tuna salad, that would be great."

He stalked out of the room and Maryse flopped back on the bed a minute, enjoying a moment without someone staring at her. Being detained was hell on introverts. She eyeballed the television remote that Stepford had left on his chair. The bedpan was still within reach so she went to work trying to snag the remote.

It took a couple of tries, but she finally managed to drag the remote off of the fabric-covered chair and onto the floor. From that point, it was easy to drag it across the tile. When the remote was close to her feet, she tackled it like a starving man on a cheeseburger.

Fox News, NBC News, CBS News.

Good God! Was there anything left on television besides the horrible things people did to one another? Life was already full of reality. What she wanted was a distraction. Finally, she flipped to a repeat episode of *Hell's Kitchen*. That would work. She liked food and she liked people who yelled, so it was a win-win.

She shoved the remote under her pillow and leaned back to watch.

She was just getting interested in the episode when Stepford returned with her lunch/dinner and placed it on the bed next to her. He closed the door, then released her from the handcuffs before perching in his chair again. Then he noticed the television and frowned.

"Where is the remote?" he asked.

"Somewhere you don't want to get caught looking or my husband will shoot you." If she never saw another newscast again, it would be too soon.

"I'm not watching this crap."

"Then look out the window or stare at the floor. But unless you shoot me, you're not getting the remote. You don't have the good taste to use it properly." She lifted the bread of her sandwich. "Is this tuna salad?"

His jaw flexed as he gave her a nod. She tore open a bag of potato chips and dug in, savoring the salt and washing it down with a soda. Stepford sat in stony silence, still glaring at her. Just when she was starting to not hate life altogether, the door opened and Ross walked in.

"There goes the neighborhood," she muttered.

Ross strode over to the bed. "You and I are going to talk."

"I can't wait."

"How did you get to the pond?"

"I drove."

He raised an eyebrow. "The truth—how refreshing. We found your truck. If your business was as legitimate as you claim, why did you camouflage your vehicle?"

"Because I don't want anyone to steal it."

"And vehicle theft on barely used swamp roads is a big concern in Mudbug?"

"It concerns me."

"I don't believe that for one minute. What I believe is that you and your accomplice were trying to spy on my investigation."

"I'm a botanist. I don't spy. I study."

"Studying my crime scene is considered interfering with a federal investigation."

"I didn't see any posted signs...no police tape. You expect me to stay off of my own property?"

"I expect you to stay away from me. I know exactly who you are, and I know Raissa is a friend of yours. I also know you like to meddle in police business."

"That's where you're wrong. I don't like to meddle at all, and if you guys did your job, I wouldn't have to be so pushy."

Ross's face reddened and beads of sweat began to form on his brow. He lifted a hand and rubbed his forehead.

"Headache?" she asked. "Maybe you hurt your head when you fell and discharged your weapon without cause."

"I did not fall! Something hit me."

"Really? What was it?"

"I didn't see it."

Maryse raised her eyebrows. "The marsh grass was only a couple feet high. I don't know of any living creature that could take a grown man down and leave no sign of passage. Maybe you should think about hitting the gym. Age can catch up with you."

Ross's nostrils flared out as he sucked in air. "What I need is for you and your meddling friends to stay out of my business, and if you don't, I'm going to make things very difficult for all of you."

"Is that a threat?" Luc stepped into the room and gave Ross a look so stern it had him stepping back from the bed.

Maryse jumped off the bed and threw her arms around her husband. "Thank God you're here. They bruised my arm, took my cell phone, tortured me for hours with CNN, and refused to feed me. Then this idiot tried to poison me." She released Luc and pointed to Stepford.

"That's a lie," the agent said as he jumped up from his chair. "I brought you perfectly good food from the hospital cafeteria."

"You brought me tuna salad. I told you I was allergic to mayonnaise."

"You lying bi—"

Luc took a step toward him. "If you want to continue breathing, you're not going to finish that sentence."

Stepford's mouth slammed shut and he took a step back.

"Is my wife under arrest?" he asked Ross.

"Not at this moment. I have more important things to worry about. But if my boat isn't returned by tomorrow morning, I'm going to charge her as an accessory to its theft."

Maryse whirled around to face Ross. "I didn't—"

Luc put his hand on her shoulder and squeezed. "Not now."

It took some restraint, but Maryse managed to keep quiet.

"Then we'll be going," Luc said. "But get one thing straight—if you ever touch my wife again, even to shake her hand, or detain her without notifying me, FBI or no, I'll pin your balls together with your badge. Are we clear?"

Ross's eyes widened a bit but apparently, he took Luc at his word.

"Let's go," Luc said and tugged her shirtsleeve.

"I can explain," Maryse said as they left the hospital.

Luc shook his head and didn't say a word—not while they walked to his truck or on the entire drive back to their home. Maryse had never seen her husband so angry and knew that although he'd been furious with Ross for the way he handled the situation, the largest part of his anger was with her. And no matter her good intentions, no way was he going to find merit in spying on the FBI with Helena in tow.

Seven hours and a mere bag of potato chips later, she had to admit she couldn't find any merit either.

After he pulled to a stop in their driveway, he exited the truck and went into the house without so much as a backward glance. Maryse climbed out of the truck and slowly made her way inside, certain the volcano would erupt once the front door was closed.

As she stepped inside and stood in the living room, Luc stormed into the kitchen and grabbed a bottled water from the refrigerator. Oh yeah, he was definitely mad. But more importantly, he looked scared, and if anger was a scarce thing with Luc, fear was practically extinct.

Guilt washed through her in waves.

Why had she been so stubborn? Luc had never asked her to do anything without a reason. Why hadn't she trusted that the man who loved her more than anything had a valid reason for asking her to stay out of the swamp?

He stared out the kitchen window for what seemed like forever. The sound of the kitchen clock ticking was the only thing that broke the silence. Finally, he turned around to face her.

"Do you realize how bad things could have been if someone besides Agent Ross had walked up on you?"

"No," she said honestly. "I don't realize how bad things could have been because you won't tell me anything."

"Is my word not good enough for you? Do you really trust me so little?"

Maryse's gaze dropped to the floor. He'd hit her exactly in her guilty spot. "I never thought about it that way. I just wanted to help find Raissa."

Luc ran one hand through his hair. "Look, I get it. I want Raissa found as much as you do. I'm not trying to diminish the seriousness of the situation, but you're not a trained detective. Even if there were no risk from my end of things hanging over you, it would still be dangerous for you to insert yourself in the middle of the investigation. Someone kidnapped a federal agent and tried to kill another. Do you think they'd even blink at doing the same or even worse to you?"

"No, I guess not," Maryse said, the enormity of the situation crashing into her like a tidal wave.

Luc crossed the living room and lifted her head with one hand so that she looked directly at him. "I love you more than life itself. If something happened to you, I don't know how I'd make it."

Tears filled her eyes and she threw her arms around her husband. "I'm so sorry. I didn't mean to make you worry or think I don't trust you."

He pulled her close and kissed the top of her head. "I know you didn't. And part of the blame is on me. I should have given you more information."

"I know you can't tell me things, and that's something I have to learn to live with."

"That's true, but this is different. This time, the potential threat was toward you. I should have bent the rules and told you more. In that sense, I guess I didn't trust you either, and I was wrong. I'm sorry."

Maryse released him and he wiped the tears from her cheeks with his fingers. "We're two sorry people," she said, managing a small smile.

"Everyone can improve," he said and motioned to the couch. "I'd like to tell you why I'm so worried. If you still want to know."

"Of course!" Maryse sat in the middle of the couch and Luc dropped next to her. He was silent for several seconds, staring out the living room window and into the street, then finally he cleared his throat.

"Remember six months ago when I was gone for a month?"

"How could I forget? It was the longest thirty days of my life."

He smiled. "Even longer than the first time Helena showed up?"

"Okay, the second-longest thirty days of my life."

"I was working undercover on a big drug case in New Orleans.

The supplier is a real piece of work. He targeted middle school and high school kids. Got them hooked on meth."

Maryse's hand involuntarily flew up to cover her mouth. "Oh my God."

"Yeah, he was smart about it, too. Picked wealthier areas where the kids would have plenty of disposable income but parents who were too busy working or traveling to give them much attention. He used kids to do the dealing, so it made it even easier to convince the others to use."

"And once they tried it..."

"They were hooked. Go too long without it and the kids would fall into a state of depression that they couldn't handle."

"So they'd go looking for more drugs."

Luc nodded. "After a couple of deaths in the same school district, the DEA went in to try to identify the supplier. With the middle school's approval, I took a position as a substitute teacher."

Maryse stared at her husband. The husband who, like her, wasn't convinced he ever wanted kids. "How'd that work out for you?"

"Ha. Yeah, in some ways, it was the hardest undercover case I've ever worked. But I managed to spot the dealers quickly and since they were young and unseasoned, it wasn't hard to track them back to the source. I reported all my findings for a month and then at the end of thirty days, the DEA made the bust."

Maryse shook her head, slightly confused. "I don't understand. It sounds like everything went well. And that was six months ago, so why is it a problem now?"

"Because Antonio Rico, the head of the supply chain, made bail right after his arrest, then instead of heading straight for his attorney's office to plan his defense, he launched his own investigation to figure out who the narc was. Word has it that Antonio is not all that stable and is hell-bent on revenge."

Maryse felt her chest constrict. "Does he know it was you?"

Luc nodded. "We think so, and to make matters worse, no one has seen him in over a week."

"And you think he may come after me to get to you."

Luc nodded. "The wife and children of another agent on the case disappeared two weeks ago, and they still haven't been found."

Maryse's heart pounded in her temples and she felt slightly dizzy.

"We have no proof that Rico was involved," Luc continued, "but we have no other viable suspects." Luc reached over and clasped her hand. "I am so sorry about this. I never thought my work would come back on me like this, much less you."

Maryse sucked in a breath and slowly blew it out. "You see it in movies all the time, but I always figured it was just a plot device...you know, something that didn't really happen that often."

"It doesn't. Most criminals are more concerned with getting a not guilty verdict. Seeking revenge on federal agents will only buy them more trouble and they know it, but apparently Rico is not your garden-variety criminal."

"Jesus." Suddenly the room felt hot and cramped.

"Do you have any idea what I thought when Agent Ross called and said he'd found you in the swamp?"

She sucked in a breath. "Oh no. You must have thought...I mean, given the circumstances, you thought he meant a body."

Luc nodded, looking miserable.

Maryse teared up again, horrified that her own stubbornness had caused her husband such pain. "I don't know what to say except I'm sorry. And I promise I will keep concrete beneath my feet and try to stay in plain sight of others. I can move my computer and some of my equipment to the hotel and work there until you think it's safe."

Luc leaned over and kissed her. "I hate for you to change up your entire routine, but I'd be lying if I said that wouldn't take a load off my mind."

"Can you help me move some stuff tomorrow morning?"

"Absolutely."

"So, uh, do you want to know what I was doing?"

Luc shook his head. "I think I already have a good idea, and I assume you didn't get anything useful or you would have already blurted it out by now. Although I do admit to being slightly curious about the boat theft part of the accusations."

"Helena stole the boat."

"Why did I know that's what you were going to say?"

"Because it's Helena."

"True. So where is she now?"

"I have no idea." Maryse bolted upright. "Crap. We forgot to get my cell phone from Stepford."

"Stepford?"

"Stepford Agent—the man who was guarding me."

Luc smiled and moved closer to her. "I'll get it tomorrow. Now, if the fighting is over, can we move to the making up part?"

"I thought you'd never ask."

CHAPTER TEN

JADYN TRUDGED behind Colt as they left another empty camp behind them. Daylight was fading quickly, and she knew they didn't have time for much more searching.

"Maybe we could use flashlights and keep going," she suggested.

Colt stopped and looked at the sun sinking over the line of cypress trees. "I've thought about it. We could, but we might miss signs of recent entry using only flashlights."

"True, but at least we'd know if the camps were empty. Most of them had electricity."

"Most of the ones we saw today did, but our next group moves us farther into the swamp and that area doesn't have power. The owners use generators for electricity, but they usually take them with them when they leave to avoid theft. I guess I should have planned better and had us start with those first."

"No second-guessing yourself now. Besides, we both agreed it made more sense to start with camps nearest where you found the car."

He nodded and glanced once more at the disappearing sun. "If you don't have a problem with the conditions, I wouldn't mind checking out more."

"I definitely don't mind. If we see anything suspicious, we can always recheck that location tomorrow."

"Sounds good." He stepped into the boat and fished two flashlights out from the seat storage. Jadyn clutched the flashlight and took a seat. It was the right thing to do, continuing their search as long as they were alert enough to do so, but it was also more dangerous. Once the sun went down, the traffic on the bayou would dwindle down to only the die-hard midnight fishermen, and without the general buzz of local boats, someone would be able to hear their boat coming from miles away.

Whoever was brave enough to kidnap a federal agent wouldn't have any trouble opening fire on local law enforcement.

"That was the last camp in this section," Colt said. "We need to backtrack a bit to get farther east, but with any luck, we'll be able to check everything else west of the pond tonight."

Jadyn nodded and settled in for the ride. Based on what she'd gleaned from the maps, it would take a good ten minutes to wind out of the area they were in and get to where the next section of camps started. Ten minutes for her to consider everything that could possibly go wrong with this plan. She shook her head. What she needed to do was shift her focus to something that could occupy her mind but not stress her out.

Like Helena Henry.

She couldn't even imagine what all had transpired between Helena and the FBI agents, and God help her, she was dying to know. The fact that Helena had left Maryse behind worried her a bit, but if anyone could traverse the bayou without being sighted it was Maryse. Worst case, Ross detained her and would have to let her go. After all, he could hardly arrest her for being on her own property.

Colt slowed the boat and Jadyn peered into the dim light at

the bank, barely making out the outline of a camp about twenty feet from the pier.

"This one belongs to your boyfriend Bart. He inherited it from his father."

Jadyn threw her hands up. "Why does everyone keep calling him my boyfriend?"

"It's kinda obvious he's got a thing for you."

"Well, the thing has to run both ways or it doesn't equal a relationship. I barely know the man."

Colt smiled. "A picky woman. I would never have guessed."

He looked way too smug about Jadyn's denial of interest, which irritated her. "What does Bart do, anyway?" she asked, knowing her interest in the other man would take some of the wind out of his sails.

The smile disappeared. "Construction. He's a master welder and they're in high demand with all the rebuilding after Katrina."

"A master welder...so I guess that means he's good at it?"

Colt nodded, although he didn't look overly pleased about it. "The best I've ever seen except for his father."

One of the boards on the pier sagged beneath her and she shook her head. "I guess the skill set doesn't transfer to wood."

"No, that's the rule of professions—what you do at your job, you avoid at home, so I imagine most structures around Bart are falling apart."

"That's so true. My uncle is a plumber and refused to fix the leak in his bathroom. One night while my aunt was taking a bath, the tub fell straight through the floor and into the crawl space."

Colt laughed. "Talk about literally being in hot water."

"Oh, she still uses it to get her way, and that was well over ten years ago."

"I suppose there's no statute of limitations on having to crawl back into the house from your own bath."

Jadyn grinned. "I suppose not."

As they walked up the equally saggy steps to the front porch, Jadyn hoped the weak wood held long enough for them to get in and out. The door was unlocked, as most of the others had been, but with no electricity at the remote camps, except for the stream from their flashlights, they were staring into darkness.

Jadyn shone her light across the room, trying to get a feel for the layout. A kitchenette, of sorts, stretched across the back wall with a tiny table and two chairs in front of it. The wall to the right held an ancient television with an even older couch in front of it. The wall to the left contained a double bed. The entire space couldn't have been more than twenty feet square.

"This one won't take long," she said and followed Colt inside.

Colt pointed to a door in the middle of the wall on the left. "I'll check out the bathroom. Start canvassing on the right."

"Yep," she said and moved to the right, shining her light on the floor.

She couldn't see any signs of recent passage, but then the tattered rug that covered the living area was light tan and already covered with dirt. It would be impossible to determine if the footprints had been made recently or a month ago. She continued forward, shining her light across the wall with the television, and then moved to the couch.

It was covered in dark gray corduroy, a style that hadn't been popular in Bart's lifetime, so she assumed it came with the inherited camp. As her light panned over the far armrest, she took a step forward, ready to move into the kitchen area, but then she stopped.

Out of the corner of her eye, she'd seen something that didn't fit. She backed up and leaned over the couch, slowly shining her light over every square inch, trying to locate what had caught her attention. On the inside edge of the armrest she saw it—a darker spot in the fabric. She touched it with her finger, but whatever it was, it was dry.

"You got something?" Colt asked as he exited the bathroom.

"I'm not sure. This could be blood, but it's dried."

"It doesn't take blood long to dry, especially in this heat."

He stepped beside her and rubbed his finger on the dark spot. "It's flaking off a bit. If it has been here for a while, it probably would have flaked off before now, especially with Bart and who knows who else occupying the couch."

"Can we get a good sample from the flakes?"

"I'm not sure, but I'm not going to take any chances." He pulled out a pocketknife and cut a section of the fabric off the armrest, then folded it with the stain on the inside and slipped the entire thing into his front pocket.

"Won't Bart be mad about his couch?"

Colt reached for a roll of duct tape that was on top of the television and taped the hole in the couch. "There. All fixed."

Jadyn shook her head. "That's not exactly quality patchwork."

"Nonsense," he said and shone his flashlight on the opposite armrest. "Now they match."

Jadyn glanced at the other duct-taped armrest and smiled. "It's sorta nice living in a town where the keeping-up-appearances standards are so low."

"Welcome to Mudbug."

Jadyn laughed and moved to the kitchenette while Colt checked the sleeping area.

"Nothing," she said.

"Here either. Let's roll."

They exited the camp and headed back to the pier. What little sunlight had remained when they entered the camp was completely gone now, and the pitch-black swamp had come alive with the sounds of the night creatures. Something croaked as they stepped onto the pier and Jadyn drew up short, shining her light across the water.

"Was that a frog or a gator?" she asked.

"Bullfrog. Gators have a much louder rumble. One that you can almost feel, if that makes any sense."

"Yeah. I haven't been out here to work at night yet. I was waiting until I knew my way around a bit better, but I need to be able to identify the sounds."

"That's a good idea. Most of your work will happen or can be put off until daylight hours, but you never know when you will have to venture out at night. Sometimes we get a kid who doesn't listen to his parents and wanders off into the swamp."

"Ugh. I hadn't even thought about that."

"It's not as bad as it sounds—from your end anyway. The town pulls together on that sort of thing, so there's never any shortage of volunteers. All of them know these swamps like their own backyard, and we never travel in singles. Not at night."

Colt stepped into the boat and moved to the steering column. As Jadyn started to step in beside him, a gunshot ripped through the night air and a split second later, she heard a bullet whiz by her head.

Immediately, she jumped off the side of the pier opposite the shot, and sank up to her chest in the shallow water and mud. The gun fired again and she heard a large splash on the opposite side of the pier.

Colt!

A burst of panic raced through her as she worried that the shooter had hit his mark this time. She crouched behind one of the huge pylons and peered under the pier, trying to see something in the inky dark. She'd dropped her flashlight when she jumped—not that it would have done her any good soaking wet, and it would have given away her position—but she still felt more vulnerable without it. Her gun was still strapped to her waist, but the rounds were saturated and useless.

Bottom line—she was trapped.

She felt something bump against her leg and barely stifled a scream. What if that sound hadn't been a bullfrog after all? She'd seen the boat's spotlight reflecting off gators' eyes on the way to Bart's camp, the number increasing as they wound deeper and deeper into the swamp. Could she risk leaving the water? What if the shooter had a night vision scope? A second later, the water erupted and something large burst through the surface right next to her.

Before she could scream, a hand clamped over her mouth and Colt said, "It's me."

Relief rushed through her so strongly that she felt slightly weak. She clutched the pylon to keep her balance with one arm and wiped the water from her eyes with her free hand.

"Were you shot?" she asked.

"No. I dove just as the second round came. It's a good thing. I think he would have gotten me."

"Can you tell where he is?"

"Not for certain, but based on the direction of the shot, I'd say down the bayou to the right."

"Where he can sit calm and wait," Jadyn said. "We're totally screwed. There's nothing to stop him from paddling right on top of us and we'd never see him coming."

"We'd hear him, but yeah, it's not optimal." He peered under the dock. "My rifle is on the side of the boat next to the steering column. I have enough room to maneuver under the pier without getting it wet."

"It's too dangerous. He's got to have some sort of night vision to make those shots. He'll see you reach over the side."

"We don't have another choice," he said and ducked down under the pier.

Jadyn crouched lower, trying to watch his progress, but she may as well have been looking into a black hole. The sounds of lightly splashing water were the only indication she had of his passage. It felt like forever, but finally, she heard a thump, probably Colt grabbing hold of the side of the boat. She closed her eyes and said a prayer that the shooter didn't see him reach for the gun, but before she could even finish the thought, another gunshot blasted through the silence.

Involuntarily, she ducked lower and squeezed more tightly behind the pylon. Had Colt been hit? Without knowing how close the shooter was, did she dare call out?

Taking a chance, she whispered, "Colt?"

Only the sounds of swamp creatures answered her. "Colt?" she whispered a bit louder.

Again, no response.

Should she go look for him? The tide was going out. If he was unconscious, he'd be swept away from the dock and then impossible to find. Before she could change her mind, she ducked under the pier, but before she could take a step, her face slammed into something hard.

"Jesus," Colt said. "What are you doing here?"

"I was afraid you'd been shot."

"Damned close. The bullet grazed my arm as I was pulling the rifle over the side of the boat. Did I hit you?"

Jadyn rubbed her throbbing nose. "Yeah, but I'll live."

"Then let's get this show on the road before he moves closer. He can't be far away."

They slid out from under the pier and Colt crept up the bank until he could balance the rifle across the pier.

"Come as close as you can without exposing yourself," he said. "I'm going to fire in the direction I think he's in. I don't expect to hit him, but I'm hoping to scare him enough to leave. If you hear his boat fire up, then run for the camp."

"And if there's two of them?" One could easily reposition the boat while the other kept watch for any sign of movement.

"Yeah, I'm not willing to consider that."

"Okay." Jadyn wasn't thrilled with the thought either. What he suggested was very dangerous, but they couldn't stay where they were. If the shooter didn't get them, something even worse was likely to.

"Are you ready?"

"As ready as I'm getting." She moved to the side of Colt, crouched a bit in the shallow water, hoping her feet didn't sink too far into the clingy mud.

She heard Colt chamber a round and tensed, ready to spring. A couple seconds later, the shot boomed from the rifle, causing her ears to ring. Right after, a boat engine fired up down the bayou. She listened for a second as the sound got farther away.

"Go!" Colt said.

She sprang out of the water, her thighs straining to pull her feet from the thick bayou mud. When they finally pulled free, she stumbled up the bank, regaining her balance as she continued running full speed ahead. She took the steps to the camp two at a time, praying that none of the rotted wood broke underneath her, and raced across the porch and into the camp. As she slammed the door shut, another gunshot rang out.

Immediately, she bolted to the front window and peered outside, but in the dark, she couldn't see a thing. Had the shooter circled back? Had he gotten off a lucky shot?

Clutching the rough wood of the windowsill, she strained to see or hear something. Her pulse increased with every passing second until she thought her heart would burst. It's been too long, she thought. If the shooter had left, Colt would have made it to the camp by now.

She scampered back to the door, then crouched down, ready to sneak back into the dark and find Colt, but before she took the first step, the door flew open and Colt ran inside. She bolted upright as he flew by her, flinging the door shut. She reached for the lock and twisted it into place, although the flimsy metal on the thin door wouldn't be much of a restraint against anyone insistent on getting through.

"Are you all right?" Jadyn asked.

The tiniest bit of moonlight streamed in through the back windows of the camp, making it possible for her to make out his shadow, but nothing more.

"Twisted my ankle a bit coming up the bank, but it's nothing serious. Nothing compared to what could have happened."

"Is he gone?"

"For now, but we can't assume he won't come back. Let's try to find a light source and some first aid for my arm, then we need to get this salt water off our guns. We may need them."

Jadyn followed him to the kitchenette and felt inside drawers and cabinets. Her hand locked onto a round object in one of the drawers and she drew it out. Inching her fingers up the object, she located the power switch and prayed that Bart kept working batteries in it. She pushed the switch on and a burst of light shot through the small room.

"Direct it at the floor," Colt said. "We need light, but I don't want anyone to pinpoint our location from outside. We should try to find something to cover the front windows. Dark blankets, towels...anything that would help block the light."

Jadyn pointed the flashlight down and toward the sleeping area. The bedspread was dark navy and worked well to cover one of the front windows. After a bit of digging in a storage trunk next to the bed, she managed to come up with two more blankets, both dark brown. Colt hung them over the remaining front window and the one in the rear of the camp.

As soon as Colt covered the back window, she hurried into the bathroom and dug in the medicine cabinet for peroxide and bandages. Bart didn't have any stitching supplies, so she hoped that Colt's bullet nick was something the bandages could hold until he could get to the doctor.

She hurried back out into the main room and sat the flashlight in the middle of the camp, pointed up at the ceiling. The light cast a dim glow over the entire room. Colt had one of the blankets pulled back and was peering out the front window when she came out of the bathroom.

"Can you see anything?" she asked.

"No, but what little moonlight there is only appears for a couple of seconds before disappearing behind clouds again. Unless the timing was right, he could walk all the way up to the camp without my seeing him."

"But we'd hear him."

"Yeah, we'd definitely hear him, assuming he tries to get into the camp."

"You don't think he will?"

He dropped the blanket back in place and shrugged. "Nothing is impossible, but it would be foolish. All he has to do is sit across the bayou and pick us off when we exit the camp."

"Yeah, I guess so." She put the supplies on the kitchen table, fighting the feeling that the entire camp was closing in on her.

He walked over to her and put his hand on her shoulder. "I'm not saying that's what he's going to do. Maybe we surprised someone who was up to no good, and he took the opportunity to fire at us."

"You're saying it might not even be related to Raissa?"

He nodded. "It could be a poacher, a boat thief, someone who broke into this camp and bled on the couch. Plenty of stuff goes on out here that people don't want the game warden and the sheriff to know about."

"Yeah, but how many of them think killing law enforcement is a viable answer to their problem?"

He sighed. "Not many, I hope, but I'm betting the real answer would depress us both."

"Then how about we save that discussion to have over a beer at Bill's Bar?"

"Sounds good to me." He lifted his left arm up and tried to look at the back of it. "This is the one that got nicked."

She pushed his arm up a bit and saw the streak of dried blood. "Hold on a second." She grabbed a rag and wet it, then carefully wiped his arm until she exposed the injury.

"It's not bad," she said. "I didn't figure it was because it had stopped bleeding already. Just let me clean it out. All it needs is a bandage and lucky for us Bart stocked the waterproof kind, but I hope your tetanus shot is up to date."

"Working in the swamps without a viable tetanus shot would be akin to walking in an Alaskan blizzard wearing only your underwear."

An instant vision of Colt walking in a blizzard, wearing only his underwear, flashed through her mind, and she felt a blush run up her face. Horrified at her complete lapse from reality and relieved that he wouldn't be able to see her blush in the dim light, she gave a nervous laugh and reached for the peroxide and cotton balls.

"This won't take a minute," she said as she cleaned the wound. "So what is the plan? Wait until tomorrow morning, then leave? It's less of a risk in the daylight, right?"

"Yeah, but there's a small problem with that plan."

Jadyn froze, already certain she wasn't going to like what he had to say. "What problem?"

"That last shot hit the side of the boat. It was sinking fast when I ran for the camp."

CHAPTER ELEVEN

IT WAS ALMOST ten o'clock when Maryse finally called Mildred. She'd had Luc text the hotel owner hours ago that she was safe and at home, but Maryse knew Mildred wouldn't sleep a wink unless she heard directly from Maryse. And although she had every right not to care, Maryse couldn't help wondering if Helena had made it out of the swamp.

Mildred answered on the first ring. "It's about time."

"Sorry," Maryse said. "I was held captive by that ass Ross for hours, then once Luc rescued me, I got a serious butt-chewing from him."

"He's been chewing you out for the past three hours?"

Maryse blushed. "Uh, not exactly."

"I see. Well, I hope you enjoyed your marital activities while I sat here worried to death."

Maryse smiled, knowing the hotel owner was joking. "I definitely enjoyed them. Might go for a second round later on."

Mildred sighed. "Must you rub it in? Your daddy's been dead a long time."

"So find someone new. Do you really think he'd want you to sit around pining for him?"

"Maybe a little."

"Ha. You're probably right. Anyway, back to business." She gave Mildred a rundown of her and Helena's fallout with the FBI and her day with Stepford. "Did Helena make it back?"

"Yes, Jadyn and Colt found the boat drifting and out of gas. Once Colt realized the boat belonged to Ross, he decided to leave it, but he unknowingly hauled Helena back to shore."

"Wow. I wonder how Jadyn made that work."

"I can't imagine and don't trust a word Helena says. She always makes herself sound like a lot less trouble than she is."

"You haven't asked Jadyn?"

Mildred hesitated before answering and Maryse sobered, knowing something wasn't right.

"The thing is," Mildred said, "she hasn't come back just yet."

"What do you mean just yet? It's been dark for over an hour. Did you call the sheriff's department?"

"Of course, but Eugenia hasn't heard from them, either. Deputy Nelson tried to raise him on the CB, but he's not getting a response. So he went to other channels and asked the fishermen about them, but no one's seen them since late this afternoon."

Maryse clenched the phone. "Something's wrong. No matter how involved they are in finding Raissa, they would have checked in by now."

"You think I don't know that? Deputy Nelson is going over the map Colt left and getting a plan together to send out a search party tonight."

"Let me go talk to Luc." She disconnected the call and hurried back into the bedroom to wake her sleeping husband, already knowing how unhappy he was going to be with this news.

And with the fact that she had every intention of joining the search party.

"Luc." She shook his shoulder until he rolled over and opened one eye.

"You wore me out," he said. "Let me sleep."

"Jadyn and Colt haven't returned."

Luc popped up in bed. "You're sure?"

She nodded and repeated her conversation with Mildred.

Luc rubbed his cheek. "That's not good."

"I know. If they ran into boat trouble, they would have used the CB. If they needed backup, they would have used the CB. So either the CB has been disabled, they can't get to it, or they're..."

"No. I refuse to believe that. Colt's too sharp to let someone get the better of him in the swamp."

"But Jadyn is new. What if she slowed him down, or distracted him? I think they might like each other...you know?"

Luc shook his head. "I don't believe for a moment that sexual attraction is enough to reduce their concentration enough to become vulnerable. They're professionals and they're on the job."

"Deputy Nelson is putting together a search party. They're going out tonight."

Luc studied her face for a while, then sighed. "And you want to go."

"Do you blame me?"

He leaned over to kiss her gently on the lips. "Of course not. It's one of the reasons I love you so much." He jumped out of bed and grabbed his jeans. "Let me get dressed and make a couple of calls. I can probably get a couple more guys to join us."

Relief washed over Maryse. "Thank you," she said, then reached for her jeans and rubber boots.

Twenty minutes later they pulled up in front of the sheriff's department to join the crowd of fifteen or so that gathered on the sidewalk. Deputy Nelson perked up a bit when Luc stepped out of his truck. This situation was probably the world's worst nightmare for the young and mostly inexperienced deputy.

"I'm just assigning coverage," the deputy said and showed Luc the map. "If we assume they stuck to the order listed here and continued on after dark, I figure they'll be somewhere in this area. Would you mind taking the last part of it? It's the deepest in the swamp and the hardest to traverse at night, but Maryse probably knows these channels better than anyone in Mudbug."

"We'll take it," Maryse said then looked at Luc. "If that's all right."

He nodded. "I think it's best."

"Thank you," Deputy Nelson said, looking more than a little relieved. "Does everyone know their coverage area? Set your CBs to channel 19. If you see anything odd, radio immediately with your location and a description of the situation before proceeding. We don't want anyone else disappearing."

"What if they're injured?" one of the local fishermen asked.

"Radio in with an assessment and Eugenia will get either an ambulance or a helicopter to meet you at the dock."

"So you want us to move them...I mean, if they're injured?" another man asked.

Deputy Nelson nodded. "I want them out of the swamp. We're traveling in teams of two and three so that we have the strength to carry someone who may be unconscious. Do whatever necessary to get them to the dock where they can be transported to the hospital."

Everyone dispersed, heading in different directions to collect their boats and head out. Maryse was happy no one asked what to do if they found that Colt and Jadyn hadn't made it. Probably no one wanted to consider that possibility. She certainly didn't.

"My boat is docked behind the sheriff's department," she said.

Luc looked surprised. "Why isn't it at your lab?"

Maryse shrugged. "When you asked me to stay out of the swamp, I figured it was better to move it into town. I've never had any problems at the lab, but you never know." Her last four words had never been more true.

"I didn't realize you were actually trying to do what I'd asked," Luc said.

"If it hadn't been Raissa, I wouldn't have gone into the swamp. I would have continued to bitch and whine to everyone who would listen, but I wouldn't have gone there until you said it was safe. I'm not a complete butthole."

Luc grinned. "Then I guess I owe you an apology."

"I don't even care anymore. I just want to find Jadyn and Colt." She jumped into her boat as Luc untied it from the dock, then pushed them off.

"Me too," he said as Maryse flipped on the running lights.

"Do you want me to drive?" she asked.

"If you don't mind. I'd like to study things as we go."

Maryse nodded and pulled away from the dock. Luc's Native American heritage provided him with a skill set most men didn't possess. Her husband had a connection with nature and the land that defied explanation. He simply knew things—felt them in his bones. Unfortunately, he also saw things, including Helena Henry. Seeing dead people was the thing Luc liked the least about his gift. Seeing Helena made him wish he wasn't gifted at all.

As anxious as she was to get to their section, Maryse curbed her desire to fly across the bayou, letting her husband study the bank. Occasionally, he reached over the side of the boat and let his hand glide just over the surface of the water. Other times, he sniffed the night air. If such a thing as reincarnation existed, she would have bet money her husband had been a wolf in a previous life. His ability to track in the dark was uncanny.

She didn't want to interrupt his process by talking, so she kept her eye on the channel in front of her, making sure the boat was squarely in the middle, which was the safest area to travel. The night air was thick with humidity and dark clouds rolled across the sky, eclipsing the moon except for a few precious seconds at a time.

The running lights from her boat cast an eerie yellow glow on the water and she felt a chill run through her, despite the summer heat. What could have possibly happened to Colt and Jadyn that prevented them from getting home? She couldn't come up with a single answer that she liked. The bottom line was both her cousin and the sheriff were highly capable of handling most situations that could arise. Whatever detained them wasn't your garden-variety trouble.

She checked the landmarks and guided the boat down a narrow channel on the left. They were moving deep into the swamp now. The camps in this remote area could only be reached by boat, and none of them had electricity, except for the kind created by generators. The strip of camps they would check first was located on a channel that dead-ended into a bank. From talking with locals, Maryse knew that no decent fishing spots were located on the channel, so if Colt and Jadyn had run into trouble in that area, the likelihood of getting help from a passing fisherman was slim to none.

Maybe it was as simple as that. Maybe they'd gotten stranded somewhere with boat problems and the CB was also broken.

She blew out a breath. The odds of a boat owned by the sheriff's department having both engine and CB malfunctions at the same time were so low they were almost nonexistent. Maryse knew Colt kept his boat in prime condition.

"Wait," Luc said, putting his hand up. "Cut the engine."

She dropped the acceleration to nothing and turned the key to kill the engine. "What is it?"

He scanned the banks on each side of the boat, then looked up at the moon just as it slipped from behind a cloud. The moonlight swept across the swamp and his gaze followed it until he locked in on something in a channel to their right.

"There," he said. "In the shadows of the bank."

She squinted into the darkness, but all she could make out was the faint outline of cypress roots. "I don't see anything."

"He's there. I can feel him."

"Friend or foe?"

"His presence here isn't good, but I have no way of knowing if that's because of Colt and Jadyn."

"Could be a poacher?"

Luc nodded. "Let's start at the last camp on the channel and work our way back up. I'll watch and see if our friend follows us."

Maryse started the boat and glanced back as she pulled away. She still couldn't see anyone but now she could feel him, watching them. But why?

It took another five minutes of fairly slow travel to reach the end of the channel. She scanned the banks along with Luc, ready to make a quick stop if they saw any sign of Colt's boat. At the end of the channel, she turned the boat around, trying to contain her disappointment. Maybe it had been foolish to hope they'd find Colt and Jadyn on the first channel they searched, but she wasn't about to apologize for being a fool.

As she swung the boat around close to the bank, Luc grabbed her arm and pointed. She cut the engine and picked up a spotlight, directing it at the pier Luc indicated. As the light hit the running lights of the sheriff's boat, she sucked in a breath. Those lights were the only thing visible above the surface. The rest of the boat was sunken in the water and mud next to the pier.

She peered up toward the camp, unable to make out the structure in the inky black. "Do you think they're inside?"

"The logical answer is yes. The real question is, are they alone?"

———

JADYN FELT the energy drain out of her. No boat meant no CB. Not only were they trapped, they had no way to call for help. She reached for the bandages, trying to hold on to a thread of optimism.

"I told Maryse what areas we were covering today," she said. "She'll send someone for us if we don't return." Assuming that Maryse herself had returned, but she could hardly share information gained through Helena with Colt. That was one worry she'd just have to keep to herself.

"Yeah. I went over our coverage area with Eugenia and Deputy Nelson. They will rally a search party when I don't respond by radio. All we have to do is stay put until someone gets here."

And hope the shooter doesn't return and start a fire underneath them.

Jadyn pressed the bandage on his skin and nodded. "Hopefully, they'll all get together and spread out, so it won't take as long."

"I'm sure they will. The citizens of Mudbug are well-versed in swamp searches. Of course, I'm usually the one organizing the search, not *being* searched for..."

"Something different. Gives others a chance to be in charge, right?" She pulled her gun from her holster and began to dismantle it. Colt felt the bandage, then pulled out his weapon and did the same.

"I figure we can lay the rounds out on a towel to dry," he said. "We can use the tap water to rinse the guns. It's rainwater, caught in a big tank out back. It's not ideal, but it will do until we can get home and do a real cleaning job."

They worked in silence, unloading the rounds from their magazines and rinsing their guns under the faucet. The gallon jug of drinking water they'd found was set aside for personal use, as Colt described the drinking quality of the tank water as less than desirable unless one liked stomach problems.

Once they were finished with the weapons, Jadyn glanced over at the kitchenette. "I'll check the cabinets for something to eat."

"Cold beans would be better than nothing. I'd also like to wash this mud off and let my clothes dry. Were there any blankets left?"

"No. We used them all on the windows, but I saw a couple sets of sheets in that storage bin where the blankets were. Probably better anyway, given the heat."

He nodded. "Do you want to clean up first? I can do the food search."

"Sure," she said, trying to squelch the range of emotions running through her. She knew Colt was right—they needed to wash off the filthy mud and water, but the thought of sitting around with Colt all night, wearing nothing but a sheet, had her heart pounding.

"Here," he said and handed her a penlight. "I found this in one of the kitchen drawers. It's not a lot of light, but the bathroom is tiny, so it's enough."

She grabbed a towel and navy sheet from the storage bin, then headed to the bathroom. What in the world did it say about her that her heart beat equally strong imagining alone time with Colt as it did when she was being shot at? Was she really that afraid to admit just how attracted she was to the sexy sheriff? Or was she simply trying to avoid the humiliation of developing feelings for someone who didn't feel the same way?

She closed the bathroom door and clicked on the penlight, placing it on the edge of the sink. Colt had undersold the bathroom as tiny. The room was so small there was barely room to move without bumping into something. She removed her filthy clothes, tossing them into the shower for a rinse along with her, then turned on the shower and stepped into the stream of water.

The water wasn't icy, by any means, but for someone who liked her showers flesh-reddening hot, it made her grit her teeth. She hadn't seen soap, so she grabbed a bottle of shampoo and used that to clean herself, figuring her clothes would benefit from the falling residue. She hurried through the process, both because she didn't know how much water was in the tank and because she didn't want to leave Colt without backup any longer than she had to, then turned off the shower and wrung out her wet clothes as well as she could manage.

Wrapping herself in the sheet in a way that she could trust the thin cloth to remain in place required flexibility gained from yoga and memories from a college toga party attended many years ago. She finally managed a one-shoulder design that while not fashionable was functional enough to move quickly if needed and with minimized risk of leaving her exposed. Satisfied that it wasn't going to get any better, she grabbed her wet clothes and towel and went back into the main room.

Colt stood at the kitchenette counter and looked over at her with a grin. "I found cans of ravioli and a Coleman stove with propane. How does a hot ravioli dinner sound?"

Her stomach rumbled and she laughed. "Sounds like gourmet. Let me take over."

He nodded and she took over watching the cans of ravioli as he grabbed his sheet and towel and headed into the bathroom. She stirred the ravioli, pulling the bottom pasta up to the top, her stomach clenching as the smell of tomato sauce wafted up at her.

His excitement over finding something decent to eat was called for, but she figured most of it was for her benefit. Colt knew they were in a bad situation and even a porterhouse steak wasn't going to make things better. What bothered her most of all was the feeling of being trapped. She'd never been in a situation where she wasn't able to simply walk away—except for while flying, but that wasn't the same.

In Bart's camp, she was cut off from all technology, basic utility services, food and clean water, and even the means to get back to civilization without the risk of being eaten or shot. It was disconcerting and had her on edge. Every creak of the camp or whistle of the wind had her drawing the blankets aside and peering out into the darkness, wondering if the shooter was still there, biding his time.

She sighed and stirred the ravioli once more. It was going to be a long, sleepless night.

The door to the bathroom opened and she looked over in surprise, not realizing how much time had passed since he'd left the room. Colt hadn't bothered with fancy sheet dressing. Instead, he'd chosen to fold it in half and wrap it around his waist a couple of times. The result was exposure from the waist up and the top of his knees down.

But that wasn't the only result.

Her pulse quickened and she sucked in a breath, then whipped back around to the counter, hoping he hadn't seen her reaction. She'd already known Colt was an attractive man, and she'd thought his clothes did little to disguise his athletic build. But she couldn't have been more wrong.

The man behind her was some sort of Greek god. T-shirts hadn't hidden his broad shoulders and muscular chest, but they hadn't held a clue about the rippled abs or the exquisitely defined back. Short of television, she'd never seen a more perfectly designed human, and she had no doubt that if the rest of the sheet were removed, his thighs and rear would be just as lovely.

She took another deep breath and slowly let it out, trying to regain control of her racing thoughts. This was no time to act like a love-struck schoolgirl. Hormones were a fine enough thing in the proper amount and place. This was neither.

"You hear anything while I showered?"

His voice sounded right behind her, and she chided herself for being so lost in thought that she hadn't even heard him walk up.

"No," she said and glanced over at him. "Nothing but normal things, anyway. Except...never mind."

"Except what?"

"It's just a stupid personal thing."

He raised one eyebrow. "Now you have to tell me."

"I don't know," she said as she looked down at the ravioli. "I guess it just seems that everything normal sounds kinda sinister, like Mother Nature is on high alert."

She looked over and saw him staring at her, frowning.

"I'm not crazy," she said.

He smiled. "I know you're not, but what you've got is really good intuition. It's a rare gift and a good one to have in law enforcement."

"You're saying you feel it too?"

He nodded. "It's not as strong now as it was earlier, but I can still feel it—that niggling at the back of your neck that the threat is still out there."

Jadyn grabbed a rag and removed the two cans from the stove and poured the contents into Styrofoam bowls. "Do you think we're right?"

They grabbed the bowls and plastic forks and took a seat at kitchen table, both silent for a couple of minutes while they dug into their dinner.

"Yeah," he said finally. "I think we're right. When I first joined the police force and got feelings like this, I thought it was fear and inexperience that caused them. And every time I ignored the feeling, I came dangerously close to serious trouble, even death. That intuition is not something I ignore any longer, nor is it something I'm ashamed of, even when I've been called chicken by other officers for not walking into questionable situations."

Jadyn nodded. "It's a relief to know it happens to someone else. Someone who's not crazy, that is."

He grinned. "Who says I'm not crazy?"

She smiled, then thought about the shooter. Was he crazy or calculated? They presented different problems, but calculated was sometimes predictable if you could figure out what they were after. Crazy was a whole different story and a lot more dangerous. Suddenly, she remembered the sample Colt had cut from the couch and she straightened in her chair.

"Oh no," she said. "The sample with the blood is ruined from our dip."

"No big deal. I didn't cut away the entire thing. I'll just cut off another piece before we leave."

She studied him while he devoured his ravioli. He said it so casually, as if they were having breakfast at the café and could walk out and to their homes at any minute. How did he get so calm, so centered? Was it his work on the New Orleans police force? Or just lots of experience in dangerous situations?

If that was the case, then Jadyn decided she'd rather remain jumpy. In her opinion, living the mess she was in now over and over again wasn't worth the gain. She'd always known her job would hold some element of danger, but what she'd experienced so far hadn't been on her radar and certainly hadn't been taught in her college courses.

She picked the last of her ravioli from the bowl and washed it down with the remainder of her cup of water. "Dinner was great," she said, "but I think you owe me something better for getting shot at."

He grinned. "You owe me. I'm your employee, remember?"

"That's right, then the dishes are all yours."

He rose from the table, tossed the two empty bowls in the trash along with the plastic cups. "Any other duties you'd have me perform?"

Her pulse ticked up a notch and she hoped her thoughts weren't conveyed on her face, because the first thing that came to mind was something she'd never ask an employee to do, even a sort of fake one.

"I guess that's it," she said, trying to sound nonchalant. "Should we do a watch schedule?"

He raised one eyebrow. "You planning on sleeping?"

She sighed. "No. I wouldn't be able to manage a minute."

"Then I suggest we retire to the living room."

"One minute," she said and retrieved another sheet from the storage bin. She tossed it over the couch, covering the entire piece of furniture.

"You afraid Bart has cooties?" Colt's voice sounded right next to her.

"Everyone has cooties," she said. As she turned to look at him, she realized just how close to her he stood. Her pulse ticked up another notch as her gaze swept down his perfectly chiseled chest.

He dropped his hand to her bare shoulder and set her skin on fire. "We're going to get out of this. I promise you."

"I hope our clothes dry first. Otherwise, it's going to be an odd rescue picture in the *Mudbug Gazette*."

He looked her up and down and smiled. "At least one of us looks good in a toga."

"Yeah, but I think women may argue about which one." The words flew out of her mouth unbidden, and the mortification was right behind. Not since she was a teenager had she said anything so embarrassing.

And true. Which was completely beside the point.

Colt's eyes locked on hers and his hand moved up to stroke her neck. When he leaned in, she knew he was going to kiss her.

CHAPTER TWELVE

NEVER IN HER life had she wanted something more, and when his lips brushed against hers, her body exploded in a tingling frenzy. Such light contact had flooded her with emotions she'd never felt before—emotions so strong they frightened her as much as they excited her. He pulled her closer to him and deepened the kiss. Through the thin sheet, she could feel the heat coming off of him and a flush ran through her, setting her entire body on fire.

You have to stop!

Her mind shouted out in desperation, but her body refused to listen and pressed closer to him until his bare chest touched her thinly clad body. He groaned and wrapped his arms around her, then began kissing her neck, working his way down.

And that's when she heard the voices outside.

"Colt! Jadyn! Are you in there?"

Colt jerked his head toward the window and released her. Cool air passed over her as he moved away and to the window.

"It's Maryse," Jadyn said as she hurried up to join him. "I'd know her voice anywhere."

She peered out the window and watched as two flashlights

bobbed up the path from the deck. "I can't make out who's with her but she doesn't sound like she's under duress."

Colt nodded. "I'd like them to move in a little closer first. "

"Colt! Are you here?" a man's voice boomed out of the darkness.

Colt let out a sigh of relief. "It's Luc."

He opened the front door and yelled out. "We're here and it's safe."

Maryse broke into a run and took the steps two at a time. She barreled into the cabin and grabbed Jadyn in a hug so hard, she might have bruised a rib.

"Oh my God!" Maryse said as she clutched Jadyn. "We were so worried. I was afraid..."

"I know," Jadyn said.

Maryse released Jadyn and sniffed, then finally caught sight of Jadyn's wardrobe. She stared for a moment, then turned to gawk at Colt, apparently struck speechless. Luc, on the other hand, had no such issue.

"Fancy uniform," Luc said, grinning at Colt. "Is that the new sheriff department issue?"

Colt laughed. "I don't think I'd want to work in the swamp wearing this getup."

"I don't know," Maryse said. "You'd probably run into more trouble on Main Street with that getup. We saw your boat sunk next to the pier. What happened?"

As Colt filled Luc and Maryse in on everything that had happened, Jadyn reassembled their firearms. Luc occasionally stopped Colt to ask a question, but Maryse stood silently, her expression growing more and more troubled as the story progressed.

"Did you get a look at the shooter?" Luc asked.

"No," Colt said. "It was too dark."

Luc frowned. "You two were lucky—damned lucky. If you

hadn't moved just when you did or if he was a better shot, we wouldn't be having this conversation."

"I know," Colt said. "Man, you don't know how happy I am to see you guys. We figured we were stuck here for the night."

"Is it safe to leave?" Jadyn asked. "He could still be out there."

"I think he is, or was," Luc said and told them that he'd gotten a glimpse of a boat hidden close to the bank.

Maryse bit her lower lip. "Do you think he'll try again?"

Luc shook his head. "He's not going to get the chance. I'm going to radio all the others and get them over here. One man can't take out a caravan. I'll be back in a minute."

Colt grabbed his clothes from the back of the kitchen chair and headed for the bathroom. "Let me throw on my clothes and I'll be right behind you." Less than a minute later, he was hurrying out of the camp after Luc.

"So," Maryse said as she watched Colt shut the door behind him, "quite a body on our sheriff."

Since Jadyn had just been thinking the same thing, she knew better than to look Maryse in the eye. "Aren't you married?"

"Yep, as married as last time you asked me. And still not blind."

Jadyn sighed. "Yes, he's got quite a body."

"It looks really good in a sheet. How does it look without one?"

"I don't...we didn't. Jeez, Maryse!"

Maryse shook her head. "That's disappointing. In the movies the hero and heroine always have sex when they're about to die. Hell, come to think of it, the first time Luc and I had sex we almost died right after."

"Seriously? Now that sounds like a story worth telling. Much more interesting than Colt and I wearing sheets and eating ravioli while our clothes dried."

Maryse grinned. "As soon as things are back to normal, I'll tell you over dinner and a beer, but you're buying."

"It's a deal. I guess I better go change myself."

"Unless you plan on riding home like that."

Jadyn headed to the bathroom and shed the sheet. The clothes were still wet, so she skipped the undergarments. She had some difficulty getting on her damp jeans but finally managed to pull on her clothes and boots. The rest she carried back into the main room and shoved into the trash bag along with the ammo and holsters. She picked out the driest of the rounds, reloaded magazines for both her and Colt, and shoved her firearm into her waistband.

"Do you think the rounds are dry enough?" Maryse asked.

"Yeah. They should be fine."

Maryse started to say something but before she got a word out, Luc and Colt came back in the camp.

"Four boats were within twenty minutes of here. The first two are only ten minutes out. We'll head out when they arrive. The others won't be far behind them."

Jadyn nodded, her desire to be back safe in the hotel with Mildred fawning over her almost overwhelming her. It was a strange feeling for someone used to being on her own, but also a welcome one.

"Can you ask dispatch to call Mildred?" Jadyn asked Luc.

"Already did it," he said.

"Thanks," she said. "I didn't want her to worry any longer than she had to."

"Ha," Maryse said. "She'll worry about us until we're all back in Mudbug, showered and in our beds."

A spotlight flashed through the doorway and three blasts from a marine horn sounded.

"We will be shortly," Luc said. "Get your stuff and let's get out of here."

Jadyn grabbed the trash bag with their supplies, their ammo and some of their undergarments, and turned to follow the others out.

"Wait!" Colt drew up short. "The sample from the couch."

He pulled out his pocketknife and cut the remaining bloody section off the couch, then grabbed a Baggie from the kitchen and locked it inside.

"What's that?" Maryse asked.

"We found blood on the arm of the couch. We wanted to test it, in case..."

Maryse nodded but Jadyn could see how troubled her cousin was at the thought of something bad happening to Raissa.

Jadyn was troubled too, but not only about Raissa.

At the pier, Luc quickly filled the other men in the search party in on the shooter. There were several exclamations and a couple of muttered threats against the perpetrator, but all seemed to understand the importance of returning in a group and the imperative to keep a close watch the entire time.

Since they had no reason to assume the shooter had targeted them personally, Jadyn and Colt both rode with Luc and Maryse third in the troop of four boats. The party pushed up the bayou as quickly as possible, all eager to get back to the safety of the town. Jadyn sat on the rear bench with Maryse, who directed a spotlight at the bank as they passed. Jadyn had no doubt her cousin was looking for Raissa, and her disappointment at the failed search increased.

Suddenly, Maryse jumped up from the bench and grabbed Luc's shoulder. "Stop!"

Luc held up his hand to alert the boat behind him, then cut the power on the boat. "What is it?"

"I saw something on the bank. Something white." She lifted the spotlight and cast it across the bank behind them. "See there, just inside the tree line."

They all peered at the lump of white that was illuminated by the spotlight.

"I can't tell what it is," Luc said. "I'll pull closer."

He yelled out his intentions to the other search party members and asked them to stay put, then carefully directed his boat to the bank.

Colt jumped onto the bank, drew his weapon, and headed for the lump of white. He leaned over the lump then sprang back up. "It's Raissa!"

Maryse clutched Jadyn's arm. "Is she alive?"

"Yeah, but we need to get her to the hospital fast."

Luc jumped out of the boat and went to help Colt lift Raissa. Maryse grabbed the CB and called the sheriff's department dispatch, asking them to send a helicopter to meet them at the dock. While she called, Jadyn dug some life vests from beneath the bench and made a bed of them across the bottom of the boat.

A couple seconds later, Colt placed Raissa on the vests and Luc took off, slowing only to tell the men that Raissa was found and injured and to move as quickly as safety allowed. Jadyn sat beside Maryse in the bottom of the boat next to Raissa and checked her vitals. Her pulse was weak but steady, her breathing shallow. Her wrists were marked all the way around and had bled in some places. Jadyn lifted her pants legs and found the same marks around her ankles.

But the most distressing thing was the purple lump on the side of her head.

Clearly, she'd been conscious when she escaped, probably losing her captors in the swamp, but had the head injury caught up with her and caused her collapse? And was there permanent damage?

Two unconscious FBI agents, and no hard facts as to why.

She could only hope that Raissa awakened soon and had some answers.

———

JADYN WAS in the midst of a dream where she and Colt were stranded in a camp, but this time, his sheet was gone and he hadn't been stopped at a single kiss. He had just ripped off her toga when someone started knocking at the door. Seriously?

It took her several seconds to realize that the scene with Colt was a dream and that someone really was banging on her hotel room door. A second later, she locked onto Mildred's anxious voice and popped out of bed, flinging open the door.

"What's wrong?" she asked.

"Raissa is awake! We need to get to the hospital. And keep it quiet, if you can. I'd like to get out of here without having to deal with Helena. I'll tell her when we get back."

Jadyn waved Mildred inside the room while she threw on jeans, T-shirt, and tennis shoes. "Won't Agent Ross be there?"

"He's on his way, but Raissa has already made it clear to her doctor that she will not speak to the FBI until she speaks to her friends."

"But I've never even met her."

"Doesn't matter. Maryse and I want you there. Raissa would too if she'd already met you, especially after what you risked searching for her. So hurry up. I've called a friend to cover the front desk for me."

Jadyn pulled her hair back in a ponytail and grabbed her weapon and wallet. "What are we waiting for?"

Mildred hauled butt downstairs and grabbed her purse off the front counter, nodding to an older woman with curly gray hair. Jadyn had to pick up her step to keep up with the hotel owner and knew Mildred was anxious to see for herself that Raissa was alive and well. Once she'd been admitted to the hospital the night before, the staff refused to let anyone see her and they'd all gone home, worried but hopeful. The fact that Raissa was awake and talking was the best news Jadyn could have possibly awakened to.

Jadyn had planned on driving, but before she could pull her keys out of her pocket, Mildred jumped into her still-dented car and waved frantically at her. Not wanting to hold things up any longer than she already had, Jadyn hopped into the passenger's seat.

Mildred's anxiety extended to her driving and Jadyn cringed as the older woman barreled down the highway at a good twenty miles per hour faster than her normal speed, especially since Jadyn was well aware the air bags were currently missing in Mildred's car. In between worrying that Mildred would get them to the hospital safely, Jadyn wondered what Raissa had to tell.

Would she remember everything that had happened? Lots of times people had lapses of memory when something traumatic happened. Granted, Raissa was better qualified than most to handle extreme pressure, but those marks on her wrists and ankles were no joking matter. Whoever had held her was cruel, and Jadyn worried about what else they'd done to her.

When they reached the hospital, Mildred practically jumped out of the car before the engine died, and Jadyn rushed after her. They stopped short in the waiting room, and Jadyn whistled, taking in the two sides of the room, divided for war. On one side was Mildred, Maryse, and Colt. On the other was Agent Ross and three of his minions.

"You're out of line," Ross said to Colt. "This is my case and Raissa is my witness."

Colt's jaw flexed and Jadyn could tell he was beyond angry. "More importantly, she's the victim. She's specifically asked to speak to her friends first. You're welcome to go in and try to get her to talk, but I have to tell you, I don't think you'll get anywhere. She's as stubborn as the rest of us."

"You all have interfered with this investigation from the beginning."

Maryse stepped forward and stuck her finger in Ross's face. "It's a damned good thing we did, since we're the ones who found her. What have you accomplished?"

Ross sneered. "I don't answer to you."

"That's a shame, because apparently, I'm a lot smarter than you."

"Excuse me." A doctor stepped into the room, nervously glancing at the people gathered. "Ms. Bordeaux is asking for her friends. Are you all here?"

Ross flashed the doctor his badge. "No one is speaking to Agent Bordeaux until after I'm through with her."

The doctor frowned. "I'm afraid that's not possible. Ms. Bordeaux's instructions were specific, and given her precarious health, I'm not about to upset her. You can wait here until she asks for you, or I can ask her to give you a call."

The doctor turned to look at them. "I assume you are the friends she's referring to?"

"Yes," Maryse said and shot a smug look at Ross as they followed the doctor through the double doors. Jadyn didn't bother to hold in her grin and she strolled past Ross.

They followed the doctor down the hall and he directed them into a room.

The woman propped up in the hospital bed looked far better than she did in the boat the night before. More bruises were starting to form on her arms, but some of the color had returned to her face. She looked up as they entered, and smiled.

Maryse and Mildred ran across the room and hugged her, careful to avoid her bandaged head. They held one another and whispered for a bit. Jadyn shuffled, feeling like she was intruding on a private moment.

When they finally released her, Maryse waved Jadyn over and introduced her. Raissa shook her hand. "It's nice to finally meet you," she said.

Jadyn nodded. "You, too. I wish it were under better circumstances."

Raissa smiled. "No better circumstances than being alive." She looked at the rest of the group. "So who wants to tell me how I got here? The doctor wouldn't give me a bit of information other than who brought me in. An Agent Ross has apparently been insisting on talking to me, but I wanted to talk to you guys first—make sure I'm clear on the facts."

Colt stepped forward and filled her in on what had transpired over the last couple of days. Raissa listened quietly, then whistled when he was done, glancing from Colt to Jadyn. "Sounds like you two got the worst of it. Thank you for ignoring Ross's directive. He has a reputation at the bureau for strong-arming his way through a crowd to kiss the right ass. If you'd listened to him, I would have died out there."

No one said a word. They all knew she was right.

"Well," Raissa said, breaking the silence. "I guess you want to know what happened to me."

Jadyn's pulse quickened. "Do you remember?"

She nodded. "Most of it. We got a flat tire after leaving the diner. Zach had just opened the trunk, and I was still in the passenger's seat, digging in my bag for gum. Some guys pulled up on Harleys and asked if we needed help, but Zach told them no and they went on. Only seconds later, a car pulled up and I figured they were also stopping to see if we needed help."

"But they weren't?" Maryse asked.

"No. Three guys jumped out, guns blazing. One had his weapon trained on Zach, one held a gun on me through the driver's window, which was down, and the other guy came around to the passenger's side and opened the door, telling me to get out."

"Did you recognize them?" Colt asked.

Raissa shook her head. "Never seen them before, but based on their accents, they were all Creole or part. So I got out, and one of the guys starts searching the car—going through the trunk, the engine, even crawling underneath. Then he orders us to tell him where the merchandise is. We have no idea what he's talking about, and Zach tells him that."

"But they don't believe you," Jadyn said.

"Not for a minute. The guy who asked me to leave the car reaches inside and pulls my badge from my purse. He flashes it at the others and tells them we're feds, and they take Zach's gun and toss it in the swamp. Their driver gets really agitated and says he doesn't care who we are. No one is going to get him in trouble with the boss for not delivering. He tells us to turn over the merchandise and he'll let us live. We insist, again, that we have no idea what he's talking about."

Raissa took a deep breath and continued. "The driver said to put me in the backseat. That they had ways of making me talk. One of the guys clocked Zach with the butt of his pistol. Zach hit the ground, but as they shoved me in the backseat, I could see him starting to stir. The driver took off in their car and the other two got into mine. When we took off, I got low in case Zach started firing with his backup weapon."

"He fired an entire magazine," Colt said.

Raissa nodded. "While he was firing, the guy driving my car spun around. It was rocking like crazy because of the flat tire, but that didn't slow him down a bit. He drove straight at Zach. Zach reached for a magazine but he didn't have time to reload. He tried to dive out of the way, but they hit him."

Her eyes reddened with unshed tears. "The driver spun the car around again and they both laughed, then one of them clocked me with his gun and it was lights out." Her face tightened with anger. "What was the point of that? They had already gotten away. They didn't have to hit him and now he's..."

Mildred sat next to Raissa and put her arm around her. "Some people were just made mean. Don't you worry about it. I'm certain Zach is going to be fine."

Raissa smiled at the hotel owner. "Thank you."

She took another breath, then continued her story, telling them how she came to in a camp that fit the description of Bart's. She told them how two of her captors remained with her and grilled her over the "merchandise." Apparently, they'd searched the car, but couldn't find it, and they were growing more agitated as time passed. She tried, but was unable to get them to provide a description of exactly what merchandise they were looking for, which made her wonder if they even knew what they were supposed to retrieve.

She'd faded in and out of consciousness, probably due to a combination of dehydration and the head injury, but recalled all the snippets of conversation she heard—how they'd checked everywhere in the car but the merchandise wasn't there. How if they botched this job, they wouldn't get any others, and they could only stall for so long.

Colt frowned. "I don't understand why they focused on you in the first place. What makes them so sure you have what they're looking for?"

Raissa shook her head. "I don't know, but they are convinced."

"And you never got any inkling of what this merchandise is?" Colt asked.

"No, but clearly, it's worth kidnapping a federal agent and trying to kill another over."

"How did you get away?" Maryse asked.

"They got cocky. I found a beer tab in the couch—the old kind, where you pull it completely off the can. Anyway, the boss wanted to meet with them so rather than risk pissing him off with only one of them showing up, they tied my hands and feet even tighter and both left. I grabbed the beer tab and went to work on my wrists. I cut myself a bit getting the ropes off, but it was a small price to pay."

"That's the blood we found on the couch," Jadyn said.

Raissa nodded. "Unfortunately, once I was free, I had no idea where I was or how to get back to town. I knew that time of day the tide was going out, so I started following the bayou the direction of the tide, figuring it would at least get me closer to town. I underestimated how bad my condition was. I don't even remember collapsing."

"You're here now," Maryse said, "and that's all that matters."

"Except for finding those men," Colt said.

"Luc had work he couldn't get out of this morning," Maryse said, "but I'll call as soon as we get out of here and fill him in. He's going to ask around and see if the facts ring a bell with anyone. He'll call you if he gets anything."

"Excuse me." The doctor poked his head into the room. "I need to take Ms. Bordeaux for some tests."

Raissa gave the doctor a nod, then looked back at them. "That's all I've got, guys. I'm sorry it's not more."

"Don't worry about it," Colt said. "We won't rest until we find them."

Mildred and Maryse both gave Raissa a kiss on the cheek and they all filed out of the room and through the lobby, past a still-fuming Ross. No one said a word until they got to the parking lot.

Maryse laughed. "Ross is going to have kittens when he finds out he still can't talk to Raissa." Then she sobered. "Luc dropped me off. Can I get a ride with you and Mildred?"

"Of course," Jadyn said.

"Actually," Colt interrupted, "if you guys don't mind, I'd like to have Jadyn come with me. There's some things we need to check on."

Mildred squeezed Jadyn's arm. "Be careful."

CHAPTER THIRTEEN

JADYN FOLLOWED Colt out of the hospital, mulling over the information Raissa had given them. "So what do you think?" she asked as they climbed into his truck.

He pulled out of the parking lot and headed toward Mudbug. "I'm wondering how three men Raissa has never seen before know where Bart's camp is. It's not like it's a well-traveled area."

"True. But if you're planning on talking to Bart, you better hurry. As soon as Ross finds out where she was held, he'll be all over that angle."

Colt pressed the accelerator down a bit more. "The tests they're doing on Raissa should stall Ross long enough for us to question Bart, assuming we can find him, that is."

"What do you mean?"

"I asked Deputy Nelson for a list of the people he called last night to join the search party. Bart was called but wasn't in the party, which I thought was odd, given that he's usually the first to help with that sort of thing. When I asked Deputy Nelson about it, he said the call went straight to voice mail and that Tyler didn't know where he was."

Jadyn rolled that piece of information over in her mind. Could the likable Bart be part of something so insidious?

"I talked to him night before last in Bill's Bar," Jadyn said. "He asked a lot of questions about Ross and the investigation. I didn't really think anything of it because it seems a normal thing to do, but I suppose it could have been more than that."

Colt frowned. "After the last couple of weeks, I'm beginning to think that anything is possible."

"Deputy Nelson said Tyler didn't know where Bart was—is that unusual? I mean, they aren't roommates or anything, are they?"

"No. Bart inherited his parents' place after his dad died. His mom died of cancer years ago. About two years ago, Tyler bought an old soybean farm ten miles west of downtown. The swamp had already swallowed up the fields. If you didn't know what it was before, you'd never guess."

"What about—" Jadyn cut off as her cell phone rang. She pulled the phone from her pocket and frowned, not recognizing the number. "Hello," she answered.

"Is this Jadyn?" a woman asked.

Her voice sounded familiar, but Jadyn couldn't quite place it. "Yes, this is Jadyn."

"Hi, this is Dee, the waitress at Ted's Diner."

Suddenly, the voice clicked. "Yes, Dee, I remember."

"You said to call if I heard anything."

Jadyn tightened her grip on her phone. "And have you?"

"It may be nothing, but I had to cover for Annette on the early shift and something just happened that I think is strange. Anyway, there was this guy, Gordon Pickett, who had a heart attack in the diner last week. They hauled him off in an ambulance, and when I left early the next morning, there was a black Caddy parked right up front. I figure it had to be his."

"Makes sense."

"So a couple of days later, it was gone. I didn't think anything of it at the time. I mean, I guess I figured friends or family had picked it up for him, or maybe he wasn't that bad off and had picked it up himself. But I didn't think anything was odd about it."

"But now you do."

"Yes ma'am. Gordon showed up about an hour ago to collect his car."

"Was he confused? Maybe he'd sent someone and forgot."

"I thought that at first. My great-aunt Elise had a stroke and was never quite the same. But he insisted that he didn't have any close family or friends to send."

"Did you call the cops and report it?"

"Oh yeah. Took forever and they weren't overly polite, insisting that Gordon had probably picked up his own car and due to his heart attack, had forgotten."

"But you don't think so?"

"No. We were really slow, so I talked to him for an hour the night before he had the heart attack, and I've waited on him several times before. Except for the fact that he looked like absolute hell, I didn't notice anything different about him conversation-wise. And trust me, working the night shift, people acting different is something I pay attention to."

"That's smart."

"So anyway, I don't know that it means anything at all, but I thought it was strange, two black Caddies both disappearing from around here. I can't even remember the last time a car was stolen in this town, except for kids joyriding, of course."

"I agree. Something definitely feels wrong about all of this. I don't suppose you know how to find Gordon?"

"Sure. He gave me his phone number, in case I heard anything. Let me dig it out of my purse."

Jadyn heard some shuffling, then Dee hopped back on the line and gave her the number.

"I really appreciate this," Jadyn said as she jotted the number on the back of a business card.

"No problem, and hey, when y'all find that missing woman, would you let me know? I been thinking about her a lot lately. I mean, she was just sitting at my counter, chatting and happy, and then she disappeared. It's the kind of thing a girl's nightmares are made of, know what I mean?"

"I know exactly what you mean, and I'm happy to tell you that you don't have to worry any longer. Raissa was found last night. She's been knocked around a little, but she'll be fine."

"Oh wow! That's great. Did someone steal her car with her in it?"

"The FBI isn't giving out any information about the case, but I'm sure they won't care if we let people know she's all right."

"I'm really happy about that, especially for her aunt. Older people tend to take things so much harder. Well, I best get back to it. I'm behind busing tables after messing with Gordon and his hysterics."

"Thanks again," Jadyn said before disconnecting the call.

She slipped the cell phone into her jeans pocket and stared out the window.

"What's wrong?" Colt asked.

She repeated the conversation. "That's three black sedans stolen within the last ten days. Doesn't that seem odd to you?"

"Definitely. A place this small usually doesn't average one auto theft a year, not if you discount kids, domestic disputes, and the like." He blew out a breath. "I think we need to get that car we ran up on yesterday out of the channel, and see if there are any more with it."

He pulled out his cell phone and called Deputy Nelson, then instructed him to draft whoever and whatever was necessary to drag the cars out of the channel. When he was done explaining himself three times, he disconnected and sighed.

"Is Deputy Nelson confused?" Jadyn asked.

Colt snorted. "You could say that, and the damned shame of it is, he's the more capable of my two deputies. I inherited Deputy Simon, and have been trying to figure out a kind way to relieve him of his duties ever since."

"I might be able to help with that one. The other day, I overheard someone say they saw Deputy Simon smoking weed with the kids behind the high school."

Colt stared at her in obvious dismay. "Who said that?"

"I didn't recognize him," Jadyn hedged. "But now that you've busted the mayor's son, I bet you can get some others to talk. It might not stick in court, but it would probably be enough for Deputy Simon to gladly resign if you let it go."

"Jeez Louise. This town is going to hell in a handbasket."

"All problems with questionable personnel aside, can Deputy Nelson handle the car extraction?"

"Oh yeah. They've both had to haul things out of the bayou and know whom to contact for equipment and the like. My guess is Deputy Nelson is wondering why I'm so worried about some trash in the bayou when the mayor's son is still locked up in the jail."

A flash of the mayor and his obscenely young girlfriend raced across Jadyn's mind and she grimaced. "I guess the mayor is lying low and letting his son hang out to dry?"

"As it currently stands. Serves the little moron right."

Jadyn nodded. "So are you going to call Bart or are we just going to show up?"

"I prefer just showing up. That way, people don't have time to plan things. And as of this morning, I'm officially back from vacation, so no issues with my being in a professional capacity."

"I guess since we found Raissa in the swamp, I can claim jurisdiction. That gives us both the right to question Bart, even though I doubt Agent Ross will see things that way."

Colt slowed his speed as he pulled through downtown Mudbug, then accelerated again once they'd left the last building behind. "Ross dug his own grave over the car situation. He overreacted and now he's paying for it."

Jadyn nodded. "Is Bart's house far?"

"No," he said as he made a turn on a one-lane road. "It's about a half mile. The road dead-ends right into his place. Nothing else back here."

Minutes later, they pulled up in front of a two-story home. The clapboard siding dated the house, but it had a fresh coat of paint on it and after seeing the state of his camp, Jadyn was surprised that the lawn and building were neatly kept. A large metal shop stood about thirty feet to the side of the house with Bart's truck and an enclosed trailer parked nearby.

As they climbed out of the truck, the door to the shop opened and Bart stepped outside. He stopped short and his eyes widened, then he quickly recovered and headed their way. "You two are out and about early. You still looking for Raissa?"

"No," Colt said. "We found her last night. She's a little banged up but will be all right."

Bart brightened. "Ah man, that's great news. Was she in the swamp?"

"Yes. We found her collapsed on a bank after she'd escaped from her captor. She was being held in one of the remote camps."

Bart nodded. "Probably the least occupied given the heat right now."

"She was held in *your* camp," Colt said.

Bart's eyes widened and he looked back and forth between Jadyn and Colt. "No! That's not possible. I mean, I guess it's possible, but..." A flash of fear washed over his face. "You don't think I had anything to do with her kidnapping, do you? I haven't been to that camp in months, maybe half a year. I swear to you!"

Colt studied him for several seconds. "Someone shot at Jadyn and me last night when we went to leave your camp. Sank my boat and left us stranded."

Beads of sweat began to form on Bart's brow. "Probably someone hunting out of season."

Colt raised an eyebrow. "At night? Deputy Nelson put together a search party last night. He says he called you but your phone went straight to voice mail."

Bart stuck his hand in his jeans pocket and pulled out his cell phone. He fumbled a moment with the power. "I was working on a job last night. I turned it off so I wouldn't be interrupted and must have forgotten to turn it back on."

"Have you loaned your camp out to anyone recently?" Colt asked.

"No. I mean, everyone in Mudbug probably knows it's unlocked, but then most of the camps are."

Colt nodded. "What kind of job?"

"Huh?"

"You said you were working on a job last night. I thought all your work was in New Orleans."

"Oh...ah, sometimes I can do some prep work here. Cuts down on the time I have to be on the job site."

"Makes sense," Colt said. "Thanks for your time, and if you recall anyone who might have been using your camp, give me a call. I'm sure the FBI will close it off as a crime scene. Check with an Agent Ross to see when you can get back in."

"All right."

"Oh, and I'd expect Ross and his agents to be around here sometime soon."

Bart's eyes widened and he nodded. "Yeah, of course. Thanks for letting me know."

"No problem."

Jadyn walked back to the truck with Colt, trying to assess Bart's expressions, what was said, and what was possibly left unsaid. As she climbed into the cab, she looked over at the welder and saw him making a call.

"So what do you think?" she asked.

Colt looked over at Bart and frowned. "Seemed nervous."

"Definitely," she agreed. "I'm sure anyone would be if their property was used for a crime, but it seemed to me that his nerves were beyond just that."

"Yeah." Colt blew out a breath and pulled away from Bart's house. "But is it because of Raissa or something else entirely?"

"Wouldn't Raissa have recognized him if he was one of the kidnappers?"

"Yeah, but any number of people can be involved in moving car parts."

"He'd have to have connections somewhere else, right? Probably New Orleans?"

Colt nodded. "That would make the most sense. At least as much as any of it does."

———

COLT DROVE AWAY from Bart's house, a million thoughts running through his mind. Could a man he'd known since kindergarten really be party to kidnapping a federal agent and trying to kill him and Jadyn? Had he completely lost his ability to spot when something was wrong? Or was he simply too close to the people involved, and emotion and history were overshadowing his instincts?

He glanced over at Jadyn and clenched the steering wheel. Speaking of involvement—what the hell had he been thinking, kissing her the way he did in Bart's camp? Granted, it was an emotionally charged situation, and people had been known to do things outside of their character when subjected to that level of stress, but he knew that was bull.

The bottom line was that his attraction to Jadyn St. James hadn't lessened one bit since his self-imposed distancing. If anything, he was more drawn to her. She seemed to occupy his thoughts more the less time he spent with her. And after the kiss in Bart's camp, he knew he'd crossed a line he couldn't retreat from.

He stared down the road and blew out a breath. When all of this was over, he needed to do some serious thinking about his future, especially when it came to relationships. Because pretending that he wasn't interested in Jadyn wasn't going to work. So either he put himself out there again—risked being hurt in the hopes that this time would be different from the last—or he spent the rest of his life wondering what might have been.

His cell phone ringing brought him out of his thoughts. "It's Deputy Nelson," he said as he answered.

"I think you need to get over to the channel," Deputy Nelson said.

"You having problems getting the cars out?"

"No, sir. The road runs close by and there's a nice slope. We've got three out already and it looks like there's another one down there, but we might need a diver to get it hooked up."

"Sounds good. Then what's the problem?"

"Well, the first car was Old Man Humphrey's, like you thought. The other two didn't have plates but I had Shirley check the VIN numbers."

"And?"

"The other two cars were stolen as well. And it looks like they've been stripped down."

Colt gripped his cell phone. "I'm only a couple minutes away," he said, then disconnected.

"What's wrong?" Jadyn asked.

Colt told her what Deputy Nelson had found, and a couple

minutes later, they pulled up at the channel. Deputy Nelson waved them over to the cars, looking relieved to see them.

"We know one more is down there," Deputy Nelson said, "but we couldn't hook it. I'll call a diver." He waved at the cars. "I don't know what to make of this."

Colt walked around the cars, studying them. The interiors had been stripped, the tires and hubcaps removed, the hoods, trunks, doors, and engines, all gone. "I know exactly what to make of it. Someone is running a chop shop and this is their dumping ground. Maybe one of many, for all we know."

Deputy Nelson stared. "A chop shop? In Mudbug?"

"Someone who knows the area well enough to pick a good dumping site. No one fishes this channel since the hurricane shifted the banks. Only someone who fishes here regularly would know which channels are traveled and which aren't."

Deputy Nelson's jaw dropped. "I just can't imagine..."

"Lately, there's a lot of things going on in this town I couldn't have imagined before."

"I guess you're right, but man...what do you want me to do about the cars?"

"Haul them into town and ask Marty to store them at his garage. Tell him no access and to keep this quiet. The last thing I need is the FBI confiscating these cars and exposing our dirty laundry."

Deputy Nelson swallowed and nodded.

"Do you have the names of the other two car owners?"

Deputy Nelson pulled a piece of paper from his pocket and handed it to Colt. "That's the name, address, and phone number for all of them—at least, what's on file with the state."

"I've got to check on some things. See if you can get a diver for that last car, but don't wait on it to start hauling them to town. Call Marty and get him to start moving them to the garage. Tell him to take the back roads in and cover the cars with tarps."

"Yes, sir."

As they started back to his truck, Colt handed Jadyn the paper with the names. "Notice whose name is on there? I think we should pay Mr. Pickett a visit. See what he or the police might know about his stolen car."

They climbed into Colt's truck and Jadyn looked over at him as he started the engine.

"I've been thinking," she said.

"What about?"

"About how Tyler was ribbing Bart about not working, but Bart said he turned off his cell phone because he had work to do and didn't want to be interrupted. He's got that big shop and that enclosed trailer...wouldn't a master welder be able to easily parcel out a car?"

Colt froze and stared out the windshield. He'd been so busy thinking about how the stolen cars tied into Raissa's abduction that he hadn't spent any time trying to pinpoint who was running the chop shop. But what Jadyn said made sense. Perfect sense.

He slammed his hand on the steering wheel and cursed. How many more criminals were living right under his nose?

"We should check out his shop on the way back," she said. "Given those cars are dumped in the game preserve, I have probable cause to search. No waiting on a warrant."

Colt put the truck in gear and pulled away. "Which means no alerting anyone else as to what we're doing."

"Exactly. And if we hurry, we may be able to get it done before Ross arrives." She pulled her pistol from her holster and checked the magazine. "I hope he doesn't give us any trouble."

Colt nodded. He didn't want to think about the possibility of shooting someone he'd known his entire life. But if it was Bart who'd shot at them the night before and had a hand in kidnapping Raissa, then he wouldn't hesitate to do his job. There was plenty of time later for mourning the loss of his childhood home.

CHAPTER FOURTEEN

BART'S TRUCK and the enclosed trailer were gone when they pulled up in front of his house. Jadyn scanned the property, but didn't see any sign of activity.

"Looks like he's gone," Colt said.

"You did tell him Agent Ross would be by. Maybe he's looking to avoid that conversation."

"Well, it's not like you need permission to look around."

They climbed out of the truck and made their way to the shop. The shop had a padlock on it but Colt made quick work of it with a pair of bolt cutters he carried. They pulled open the huge swinging doors and walked inside.

Jadyn was surprised to see how neat the inside of the shop was. Toolboxes and cabinets lined one wall and workbenches lined the other. The back wall contained windows that let in natural light, and the front of the shop contained a refrigerator and tiny table with chairs. The center of the shop was completely empty.

"Whatever he was working on is gone now," Colt said.

Jadyn walked over to the workbenches and pulled out one of the plastic containers stored beneath. She pulled the lid off and whistled. It was piled high with car parts. Colt peered inside and pulled the lid of the next container, then another, and another until they'd opened all six containers.

They were all filled with car parts.

Colt stared into the container, not speaking. Jadyn had a good idea of the things roaming through his mind. She barely knew Bart but felt a sense of betrayal. The man had pursued her knowing he was committing a criminal offense on the very land she was paid to protect.

"Do you think he's the one who shot at us?" she asked.

Colt's jaw flexed. "I don't want to think so, but I can't help feeling all of this—the stolen cars, Raissa's kidnapping—are all part of the same thing."

She nodded. "I agree, but I can't make any of the pieces fit."

"Me either." He put the lid back on the container and sighed. "Let's put these back and pay Mr. Pickett a visit. Might as well collect another piece to our puzzle."

———

MARYSE AND MILDRED stood in the hotel room, their ears pressed to the wall. In the next room, Agent Ross yelled at Stepford and the other agents, blaming them for everything from failure to find Raissa first to the US inflation rate. Maryse was fairly certain when he was done, her face would remain frozen in a permanent grin. Mildred had been standing with her hand over her mouth for the last five minutes, and Maryse knew that as soon as they were back downstairs, the hotel owner would laugh until she cried.

Helena, as usual, wasn't helping matters. Because no one in the next room could hear her, she had no problem chortling so hard that she fell off the edge of the bed and rolled across the bedroom floor.

Finally, the door opened and they heard the agents hurrying past in the hallway. Maryse signaled to Helena, who stuck her head through the wall, then popped back in and shook her head.

"Ross is still in there," she said. "He's pulling out his cell phone."

"Then get back in there," Maryse whispered, "and find out what he's saying."

Maryse put her ear back to the wall as Helena walked through it, but all she could hear was the faint rumble of Ross's voice. Finally, she gave up and sat on the bed to wait on Helena. Mildred held in place for another thirty seconds and then joined her.

"It sounds like Raissa gave him the bare minimum," Mildred whispered.

"I don't think she had much more to give. She doesn't know who took her or why. She wouldn't even know she'd been held at Bart's camp if Jadyn and Colt hadn't recognized it from her description."

"I guess that's true, but I'm still glad he had to wait for us before he could talk to her. I haven't liked the man since he walked into my hotel and rented the rooms."

"That's because you have good taste."

Mildred smiled. "I'm so happy Raissa is safe. Now, if Zach would wake up, everything could go back to normal."

Maryse nodded. She was definitely thrilled about Raissa, but no matter how happy she got, Luc's worries about her safety crept through the joy and reminded her that nothing would be normal for her until the man gunning for Luc was behind bars.

The door to the next room slammed shut and a second later, footsteps hurried past on the hallway and down the stairs. Helena popped back through the wall, her eyes wide.

"Ross was on the phone with his boss," she said. "He said he'd inspected the car they pulled out of the pond, and it belonged to Raissa. They checked some number."

"The VIN number," Maryse said.

"Yeah, that's it. Then Ross said he'd spoken to Raissa but she didn't know her kidnappers. She's going to look at some books—I guess with pictures of criminals—and work with a sketch artist. They're sending him to the hospital."

"That's good," Mildred said.

Helena nodded. "His boss screamed at him so loud that I could hear him like he was standing right next to me. He said that things were out of control and he better make them right. He said Ross's future depended on it."

"Good," Maryse said. "Maybe he'll be relegated to a desk from now on. God knows, he shouldn't be allowed to work around the general public."

"Maybe he needs a rabies shot," Helena said and started laughing again. "Then Ross told his boss that if he did a better job choosing personnel he wouldn't be in this mess."

"Seriously? He's blaming his staff? What a douche bag."

"Totally," Helena agreed.

"So Ross sent his men to search Bart's camp...what does he plan on doing?"

"He told his boss he was going to sit on Bart until he got what he wanted."

"Poor Bart," Mildred said. "He can't be one of the guys Ross is looking for. Raissa didn't recognize any of them, and she knows Bart well enough."

"I'm sure Bart will have no trouble handling Agent Ross," Maryse said. "In fact, I kinda wish I could be there to see it."

"Are you going to call Jadyn and tell her what Ross is up to?" Helena asked.

Maryse nodded. "I'll call in a minute."

Mildred checked her watch and rose from the bed. "We best get moving. Visiting time starts in an hour."

"You promised I could go this time," Helena said.

Mildred sighed. "Lord help me. I did."

"Hey," Helena said, "maybe we should pick up a blackberry cobbler to bring to Raissa. I could sit in the back and hold it... maybe with some dinnerware just in case she wants to share?"

———

GORDON PICKETT WAS a short man with a bald head and a red face. Colt put him in his midfifties, and his round belly left little question as to what precipitated his heart problem.

"I'm Sheriff Colt Bertrand from Mudbug," Colt said when he answered the door. "I'm here about your car."

Pickett's eyes widened and he pulled open the door and waved them inside. "Mudbug? That's an hour from here. Did you find it? Is it okay?"

"We did find it, but I'm afraid it's a total loss." He explained to Pickett the condition of the car and where it had been found.

Pickett's face turned several shades darker and Colt wondered if he was going to have another heart attack. "What is wrong with people—stealing a man's car while he's in the hospital and then driving it into a bayou? I don't know what our world is coming to with the way kids are behaving these days."

"I don't think it was kids," Colt said. "The car had been dismantled."

"Why in the world would someone dismantle my car?"

"I believe your car was stolen by someone running a chop shop."

Pickett stared back and forth between them without saying a word. Finally, he found his voice again. "Well, I'll be damned. You say it was completely stripped?"

Colt nodded. "Everything with a hinge, the wheels and tires, and the engine are gone."

Pickett threw his hands in the air. "Well, what are you going to do? If you'll give me an address for wherever you're holding the car, I'll send someone to tow it here for the insurance adjustor to see."

"I'm afraid I can't allow that right now. The car is evidence in an ongoing investigation."

"You can't just keep my car," Pickett said, sounding agitated. "I'm the victim here. Insurance won't give me a dime until they see that car."

"I understand. My deputy is locating a secure facility to store the car as we speak. As soon as I know the location, I'll give you a call and we can work something out with your insurance agent to get him access."

"Sometime this afternoon?"

"I doubt I'll have time to make arrangements for this afternoon. My entire department is busy on a couple of investigations. It might take a couple of days before we can work something out."

Pickett glared at him a bit. "If that's the best you can do."

"It is." He pulled a business card from his wallet and handed it to Pickett. "Give me a call if you have any more questions. Thank you for your time."

"Sure," Pickett said and let them out, slamming the door behind them.

Jadyn glanced back. "I think you pissed him off."

Colt nodded as they climbed into his truck. "I meant to."

"Why?"

Colt stared at the house and frowned. "Something about him seemed off."

"The man did just have a heart attack, or something to that effect."

"Maybe." He pulled out his cell phone and called Shirley.

"I need you to run a check on someone for me," he said. "Name's Gordon Pickett. If your cousin's still volunteering at the hospital, ask her if she knows anything about him being brought in last week with heart problems. Then run a general check on the name, and get back to me when you have both. Thanks."

Jadyn raised her eyebrows. "You think Pickett's lying about the heart attack?"

"He's hiding something. He was too nervous...too agitated... but working hard to control both. They just finally got the better of him the more I stalled on the car issue." He sighed. "Maybe I'm reaching. Maybe this thing with Bart is making me think everyone is a suspect."

"That's not necessarily a bad thing."

He put the truck in gear and pulled away, unable to shake the feeling that everything was coming to a head. He just hoped when the dust cleared, that the casualties were something everyone could live with.

"Are you hungry?" he asked.

"Starving, now that you mention it."

"Then let's make a deal. We'll stop for lunch and we're not allowed to say a single word about this case."

"No argument here. My mind's on overload."

"There's a hole-in-the-wall seafood place close by. How does a shrimp po'boy sound?"

She grinned. "Better than ravioli."

Ten minutes later, they were seated at a corner table and working their way through a basket of hush puppies.

"These are incredible," Jadyn said, then popped another hush puppy in her mouth.

Colt nodded. "Just the right amount of jalapeño."

"And not gummy. If the po'boy is half as good, I may move in here."

Colt watched her as she dipped another hush puppy in ketchup and smiled. Other women he'd spent time around wouldn't have set foot in the dilapidated shack, much less complimented the food. Jadyn was different from any woman he'd ever known. She was easy to be around—competent but not demanding—and when they worked together, she was perfectly content to hang back and let him take the lead when it made sense for him to. By the same token, she had no problem stepping up and asserting her authority when it was needed.

Intelligent, hardworking, no outrageous ego, easygoing personality, and drop-dead gorgeous. Jadyn St. James might be the most perfect woman in the world.

What are you waiting for?

He took a drink of his soda. The last time he'd asked himself that question, he had all kinds of valid reasons to hold position, but damn if he couldn't recall a single one of them now.

"So," she said, "tell me something about Colt Bertrand that no one in Mudbug knows."

"Me? I'm an open book."

She shook her head. "No one is an open book."

He hesitated, trying to come up with a good response. People in Mudbug definitely didn't know his thoughts about Jadyn, but no way was he bringing that up. He had to stretch his mind a bit, but finally he thought of something he didn't think any of the locals knew.

"I like to bowl," he said.

"Bowl? As in lanes and pins and funky shoes?"

"Yeah."

She smiled. "Okay, I'll bite. Why bowling?"

He shrugged. "I sorta fell into it. I lived in a condominium when I worked in New Orleans and a group of widowers also lived in the building. They were big bowlers and were always asking me to join them. One night I did, and I decided I liked it."

She tilted her head to the side and studied him. "What do you like about it?"

"I don't know. I think because it requires enough concentration that you can't let your mind wander or you don't do well, but at the same time, it's great for decompression."

"I can see that."

"So what about you? What's your guilty sport addiction?—and no saying yoga."

She rolled her eyes. "Yoga is cliché although I have taken classes. My favorite thing, although I don't compete, is horseback riding."

"I suppose that qualifies as a sport. Did you have horses growing up?"

"God no. Mother was allergic, or so she said, and no way would she allow me to be involved in something that might make me sweat or smell. Mother had very definite opinions on how ladies should act."

"You and your mother don't seem to have anything in common."

A light blush crept up Jadyn's neck and Colt knew he'd touched a sore spot.

"We are about as different as any two people can be," Jadyn said. "I started disappointing my mother when I wasn't born on her due date and it's been downhill ever since."

"That sucks." Colt couldn't even imagine growing up with parents who didn't support and love their children. It was so different from what he'd had and his heart ached for Jadyn, who deserved so much better.

"It does indeed."

"But now you're here and have Mildred and Maryse and a host of others. They look like family to me."

She smiled. "They are the best thing about coming here. I mean, I love the job and the opportunities it gives me, but the relationships I have with Mildred and Maryse were not something I ever expected."

"You've found your place. Sometimes we have to search a

while to find it. And sometimes we have to wander a while to realize we'd been there all along."

"I can't imagine you anywhere but Mudbug."

"I can't either. Even with all the recent trouble, I know it's where I belong." He took a drink of soda. "So, where did you learn to ride?"

Jadyn seemed a bit relieved at his change of subject. "I had a high school friend with horses. I used to sneak over to his house on my mom's spa day. That way I had time to ride, then shower and primp before I went back home. In college I volunteered with an organization that teaches the disabled how to ride horses. The amount of joy they get out of the animals is incredible."

She worked with the disabled. She just surpassed perfect and is headed for sainthood.

"A couple months ago, I saw a special on equine therapy on television and was impressed," he said. "Do you miss it?"

She nodded. "Every day, but I've got a lot on my plate right now—moving here, making friends, learning a new job—it's all kept me busy, especially as the job has turned out to be a bit more than I'd bargained for."

"I'm sure it will settle down soon. Mudbug is more often quiet than rowdy."

"I hate to sound ungrateful, but I'll be glad to see the quiet side. Maybe if I get my own place with some land...who knows?"

Colt nodded. Jadyn on horseback was a vision he wouldn't mind seeing.

The waitress interrupted, delivering their sandwiches, but before he could dive in, his cell phone rang. It was Shirley.

"What do you have for me?" he answered.

"My cousin says Mr. Pickett was admitted last week suffering from a mild heart attack. He was unconscious the first time she saw him and seemed a bit out of it the time after, rambling about fishing and hunting with his cousin. They held him several days for testing but he improved, so they sent him home."

"Okay," Colt said. So far, the facts lined up with Dee's and Pickett's stories. "What about the background check?"

"That's where things got interesting. Our friend Mr. Pickett is no stranger to the police. All of the things he's been arrested for have been linked back to several of the connected families in New Orleans, but they've never been able to make any of the more serious charges stick."

"A hired gun?" Colt said.

"That's what it sounds like. And with those people as clients, it's no wonder he had a heart attack."

"True. Thanks for the information."

"There is one more thing. I thought the name sounded familiar, but I couldn't put my finger on it, so I called my aunt. You know she remembers everything."

"Yes." Shirley's aunt was well known for her long and unforgiving memory.

"Well, she said that Mr. Pickett has a second cousin from Mudbug."

"Who?"

"Buddy Anderson," she said. "There's someone at the door. I've got to run."

Colt dropped his phone on the table. Buddy Anderson —Bart's dad.

"What's wrong?" Jadyn asked.

He filled her in on the conversation, his lunch long forgotten.

"Wow," Jadyn said when he finished. "Okay, it all has to fit together somehow, but how?"

Colt stared out the window for a moment, tapping his fingers on the tabletop as an insanely wild and highly improbable scenario came to him.

"What about this?" he said. "What if Pickett was doing a job for one of the families, carrying this merchandise that the kidnappers are looking for?"

"So it was hidden somewhere in his car and he was waiting to make the drop when he had a heart attack?"

"Exactly."

She shook her head. "Talk about bad timing."

"It gets better.

"Bart passes the diner every day that he goes to work in New Orleans. What if he saw the car sitting there, not moving, and decided to take it for his little side job?"

Jadyn whistled. "Pickett calls from the hospital during one of his bouts of consciousness, and the family sends someone else to retrieve the car."

"But Bart had already taken it."

He nodded. "Then Raissa and Zach leave the diner in a Cadillac like Pickett's.

"So they see them leave the diner and decide to follow them, hanging back a bit because the bikers left right after Raissa and Zach.

"Then they come up on Zach and Raissa with the flat and steal the car." He frowned. "But that still doesn't explain why they kidnapped Raissa."

"Because they couldn't find the merchandise," Jadyn said. "Since Pickett was a hired hand, the family probably didn't know where he stashed goods for transport either. Since Raissa and Zach were FBI, they probably thought they'd confiscated the car as part of a bust and knew exactly what it contained.

"Except," Jadyn continued, "why didn't they just ask Pickett where he'd stashed the goods?"

Colt straightened in his seat. "What if he couldn't remember?"

Jadyn's eyes widened. "Because of the heart attack! He's in and out of consciousness, so the hospital won't let anyone in but family. Shirley's cousin said he was rambling, so when they do manage to get a hold of him, the information he gave them was probably confusing and sketchy."

Colt nodded. "When they can't find the merchandise in the car, they dump it, thinking Raissa and Zach already removed it. But they hold on to Raissa, thinking she'll eventually give them the goods. Since Pickett was rambling in the hospital about his fishing time with Bart's dad, he could have told them about the camp without even realizing it."

"Since they have no idea if Pickett will recover, they take advantage of the camp information and hold Raissa hostage to find out where she's stashed the merchandise, probably hoping she hasn't turned it over to the FBI yet. Raissa can't give them the information because she doesn't have it, so the whole thing stalls." Jadyn blew out a breath and flopped back in her seat. "Wow. That's thin."

"Paper thin. But it fits." He leaned forward. "Think about it—Pickett got really agitated when I told him the car had been torn down. He asked specifically what was removed, then immediately tried to arrange to have the car towed to his house."

Jadyn sat back upright. "Because based on what's remaining, he knows the merchandise is still on the car!"

"You know what this means?"

"Yeah. It means if you're not totally off your rocker, we can find the merchandise and set a trap for Pickett."

Colt smiled. "I suggest we get these sandwiches to go and head to Marty's garage. If we can find what all these people are looking for, then we'll know whether I'm crazy or not."

CHAPTER FIFTEEN

Jadyn stood next to what was left of Gordon Pickett's car as Colt pressed the lever for the hydraulic lift. The car rose slowly in front of her and stopped when there was enough room to stand underneath.

"You sure you can trust Marty to keep quiet about the cars being stored here?" Jadyn asked.

"Positive. He had a run-in with Ross at the general store today. He's not about to do anything that might make Ross happy."

She grinned. "You gotta love Ross for making our job easier." She looked at the bottom of the car. "So where do we start?"

"Based on my experience in New Orleans, I'd say let's start with the gas tank." He grabbed a wrench and went to work.

Once the tank was free, they slowly lowered it to the garage floor. The thin black box attached to the top of the tank was a dead giveaway.

"I'm looking less crazy by the minute," Colt said. He removed the box from the tank and looked at Jadyn. "Want to guess what's inside?"

"Something that doesn't ruin in swamp water...or is well contained."

"It's too light for gold," he said and he unscrewed the top of the box.

A second later, he lifted the lid off and pulled out a black bag. Even before he dumped the contents in his hand, Jadyn already knew what was inside.

"Diamonds," she said as she stared at the glittering jewels covering his palm. "Wow."

Colt looked at her and grinned. "You women and your jewelry."

She reached into his palm to pull out a good-sized diamond, then held it up to the light. "I like a well-made watch, but this stone is fit for royalty. The quality is exceptional."

"You can tell that just by looking at it?"

She put the diamond back in his palm. "Mother liked fine jewelry and she only wore custom pieces. I watched her reduce a diamond broker to near tears once."

"Are you sure you weren't adopted?"

She looked up at him and smiled. "That's the nicest thing anyone has ever asked me."

He laughed. "I bet. You ready to get this show on the road?"

"Oh yeah."

He pulled out his cell phone and called Gordon. "Mr. Pickett, Sheriff Bertrand here. Listen, we've secured a location for your car, and I wanted to give you the address. Your insurance adjuster can show up anytime between 10:00 a.m. and 5:00 p.m. to inspect the car."

He paused for a moment, listening to Gordon. "No problem," he said. "Have a good evening."

"Let me guess," she said. "Mr. Pickett is a happy camper."

"I could practically hear him dancing."

"You think he'll move on this tonight?"

"I have no doubt."

Jadyn nodded, her excitement growing. If everything went as

planned, Gordon Pickett would finally go down, and with any luck, he'd give up Raissa's kidnappers to lessen his time. They'd all be behind bars.

Then she remembered their other problem and sobered. "What about Bart? Are you going to arrest him now?"

Colt frowned. "No. Pickett is the threat. What Bart's doing is illegal, but we have no reason to suspect he's harming anyone. If I arrest him today, it might muddy the water and Pickett might stand down for the time being."

"I agree," Jadyn said. Everything he said made perfect sense, but she also got the impression that Colt was stalling. Not that she blamed him. The situation with Raissa held a positive ending as far as Mudbug was concerned—no residents were involved in the diamond smuggling or in the kidnapping—but Bart's illegal activities were just one more black mark on the small community.

One more thing that had flown right under Colt's radar.

"So how do you want to handle arresting Pickett?" she asked.

"We're only expecting Pickett. I can handle him alone."

"No way. Pickett could bring backup, or the family could send the second wave of idiots to make sure Pickett doesn't screw up again."

Colt shook his head. "Pickett won't risk telling them he knows where the diamonds are. That would be asking for the second crew to take the job out from under him. No, he'll show up alone, and I'll be ready to take him down."

"Well, you're still not doing it alone. I'll back you up."

Colt's lips quivered with a smile. "Trying to extend your jurisdiction again?"

She shrugged. "You could always ask Deputy Nelson. I'm not sure if he's as good a shot as me, but..."

Colt's grin broke through. "Twist my arm, will you?" His expression turned serious. "Thanks."

It was only one word, but Jadyn knew he meant so much

more. She wasn't just backup. She was in this with him until the very end, and she knew he appreciated and respected her for it.

Jadyn couldn't help but wonder what their relationship would look like when it was all over.

———

"I DON'T KNOW, MARYSE." Jadyn stood in the kitchen at the hotel, frowning down at her cousin, who sat with Mildred and Helena, having blackberry cobbler. The fact that it was approaching evening and both Maryse and Helena were wearing bathrobes was slightly odd, but Jadyn wasn't about to ask questions she didn't want answer to.

"It makes perfect sense to videotape him," Maryse said. "Colt said that Pickett always manages to skate by without arrest. If you arrest him breaking into the garage, that's all you have on him. He can always claim he wanted to see his car and that he had no knowledge of the diamonds. Then it's your word against his."

"One would hope the word of a game warden and the sheriff would carry more weight than that of a known-although-not-convicted criminal."

"I bet the past judges and juries had the word of cops too," Maryse pointed out. "Didn't seem to make a difference. But if you had video of him going straight for the diamonds, it would be impossible for him to argue his way out of what everyone could see. Not only that, without hard evidence, what incentive does he have to give up the other guys straight off? If you have to go to trial, it could take forever to pin down the guys who kidnapped Raissa."

"I hate to agree with her," Mildred said, "but she's right. If a jury sees him go into the garage, raise the car, and immediately remove the box and go for the black bag, there wouldn't be any possible question as to his motive. And if Pickett sees that footage first, he's far more likely to deal."

Jadyn worked to control her frustration. She didn't think Maryse was wrong—in fact, she thought the idea of video was a great one, except for the part where someone had to sit in the loft above the garage office and turn on the camera when Pickett arrived. Jadyn needed to back up Colt and couldn't do a good job from the loft. But the last thing she wanted to do was get her cousin involved in an arrest. What if something went wrong?

"It's too dangerous," Jadyn said finally. "Why can't Helena run the camera? That would give us what we want without putting anyone else at risk."

"I'll do it for another blackberry cobbler," Helena said.

Maryse rolled her eyes. "I don't doubt for an instant your dedication to acquiring more cobbler. What I doubt is your ability to turn on the camera when the time comes. What if, all of a sudden, you can't touch things? It's not like your inability to do things on command is an isolated thing."

Helena frowned. "As much as it pains me to agree, she's got a point. No matter how hard I try, I can't seem to get consistent on things, and when I'm stressed, it's even worse. And if I know there's a chance people will start shooting, I'll definitely be stressed."

"Besides," Maryse said, "how would you explain your acquisition of the video? You can't exactly parade Helena in front of a jury.

"What about Luc? Won't he be mad?" Jadyn asked, afraid she was losing the argument.

"He asked me to stay out of the swamps and I am. He asked me to stay at the hotel while he's working out of town for the next few days and I am. He might not approve of it, but this situation is not what he's worried about. Besides, I'll be way out of sight and both you and Colt will be there and armed. It's only one man. I'm sure you guys won't have any trouble taking him down."

"I don't like it either," Mildred said, "but I can't climb the ladder to the loft with these bad knees of mine, and anyone else we could trust is out of town and couldn't make it back in time. I want those bastards nailed to the wall."

The hotel owner's expression left Jadyn no doubt what Mildred would do to those men if she could get her hands on them, and Jadyn would be lying if she said she didn't want them to go down as badly as Mildred did. Zach was still in a coma, fighting for his life, and somewhere out there, the men who ran him over were walking scot-free. That made her angrier than she could ever remember being.

"I'll have to talk to Colt," Jadyn said finally.

Maryse bounced in her chair and clapped her hands.

"*But*," Jadyn said, "if he says no, it's no. I'm backing him up. I don't have any jurisdiction on this."

Maryse kept grinning. "He won't say no."

Jadyn smiled. "Just promise me you'll wear something besides your bathrobe."

Maryse drew a cross over her chest with her finger. "I promise I'll wear jeans, but as long as I've got to hang out in the hotel all day, I'm only wearing items with sashes or elastic waists."

Well, that explained the robe thing. "Has Ross been back to the hotel?" Jadyn asked.

"No," Maryse said. "But he was at the café at lunch with Stepford. We sent Helena over to check on them, but he's not up to much but grousing about his boss and bitching because he can't find Bart to question him."

"What do you mean, he can't find Bart?" Jadyn asked.

"Apparently, he hasn't been back to his house all day," Maryse said. "But then, if he's gone to New Orleans for a job, he might not be back for a couple of days."

"Ross is wasting his time," Mildred said. "Bart is a dead end."

"Ross was all pissy about him not being home," Helena said. "Put out an APB on his vehicle with orders to hold him for questioning."

Mildred shook her head. "The man is grasping at straws. It will be a wonder if someone doesn't sue the FBI before he's done making a mess."

Jadyn nodded, not about to get into a conversation about Bart. Granted, from the looks of it he had nothing to do with the diamond smuggling or kidnapping Raissa, but he was hardly an innocent. When the business with the diamonds was over, Colt still had to arrest Bart, and that was going to be a blow to these women who'd known him his entire life.

"There is one problem that I haven't quite worked out yet," Jadyn said. "Assuming Colt is okay with the video plan, that means we have to get three of us and equipment into the garage without being seen. For all we know Pickett could be watching the place already, or he could have a partner watching it for him."

"I have an idea!" Mildred popped upright in her chair. "I need to take my car in for repairs since someone flopped on top of it like a dying whale."

"Hey." Helena shot Mildred a dirty look.

Mildred put her hand up. "Try to defend yourself and you'll be digging in my Dumpster for your next meal."

Helena slumped back in her seat and stabbed another bite of cobbler.

"Anyway," Mildred said. "You, Colt, and Maryse can hide in my car. I'll drive it to the garage to leave for repair close to closing and once Marty has closed up for the night, you get out."

"What about me?" Helena asked.

"You will walk," Mildred said. "You can't ride in my car with Colt. He can't see you and you have zero capacity for keeping quiet or transparent when those without the curse are around."

"That's actually pretty brilliant." Jadyn pulled out her cell phone and headed out of the room. "Let me run all this by Colt."

She started down the hall and had just reached the lobby when Maryse stopped her. "Hey," Maryse said. "Can I talk to you for a minute?"

"Sure. Is something wrong? Are you and Luc okay?"

"We're fine," Maryse reassured her. "I am blessed to have a husband with never-ending patience."

"And he loves you."

Maryse grinned. "In spite of all the challenges I present, yes, he does."

"So what's up?"

"Actually, I wanted to ask about you and Colt."

"What about us?"

"I, uh...well, you already know I'm not exactly girlie, and God knows most things tied to emotions tend to fly right over my head—it's the scientist thing, you know? But I've noticed the tension between you two, and my limited-capacity lady parts are telling me it's nothing to do with this case."

"Is there a question in there?"

"No. Yes. Oh hell, I know Mildred and I have ribbed you some about him, but I want you to know, in all seriousness, that Colt is a good guy—one of the best. You could do a hell of a lot worse than hooking up with him. He's direct, to the point of borderline rude at times, but I have a feeling you see that as a plus. He's loyal and unless he ran wild in New Orleans, he's not a player that I'm aware of."

Jadyn's lips quivered as she tried to hold in a smile. Her cousin was so far out of her element with this discussion, but so earnest about her beliefs that Jadyn was touched. The only person who'd ever shown an interest in her love life was her mother, but she was only concerned about finding Jadyn a rich husband who would set her up for life and produce beautiful grandchildren that she could be proud of.

"You're laughing at me," Maryse said, looking dismayed. "I knew I sucked at this."

"No! I was just thinking about how you couldn't pick two worse women to have this conversation if you tried." She put her hand on Maryse's shoulder. "The truth is, I've never had people who cared about me the way you and Mildred do. My family isn't exactly traditional—or emotionally healthy, for that matter—but I'm just as rusty at this type of thing as you are."

"If you've never had people care about you, then you've been hanging out with a bunch of douche bags. You're great. Since you first arrived, you've taken everything in stride. My craziness, Mildred's mothering, Helena. Need I say more?"

"Probably not after Helena."

Maryse smiled. "Anyway, what I'm trying to say and haven't done it very well is that I want you to stay in Mudbug. And if you're going to stay, you might want a man. Colt is a good man to want."

"I get that. But I'm not sure he feels the same way about me."

"I think he does. He looks at you a certain way when you're not watching. His expression is this mixture of confusion, excitement, and fear. I think he wants to make a move, but something is holding him back."

A flash of their kiss in Bart's camp ripped through Jadyn's mind and a wave of heat ran through her.

"You're blushing," Maryse said, breaking into her thoughts. "Okay, fess up."

"He sorta made a move when we were stranded in Bart's camp...a kiss anyway, but one of those kind that make your toes curl. I think it would have gone further. At least, I don't think I would have told him to stop."

"Then what happened?"

"You and Luc showed up to rescue us."

Maryse groaned. "The worst-timed rescue ever."

Jadyn laughed. "It's okay. While I would have appreciated the action at the time, I think it would have made things awkward working together if we'd continued without thinking it out."

"I guess I can see that. Anyway, I won't keep harping on it. Go ahead and make your call."

Jadyn watched as Maryse skipped back down the hall, the ends of her bathrobe fluttering behind her. She couldn't help but grin. Her cousin was one of the most interesting people she'd ever met—a strange blend of geeky scientist and youthful spirit.

She dialed Colt's number and hoped he was feeling as energetic and creative as Maryse.

———

JADYN SCANNED the garage from the side door, making sure her and Colt's hiding places provided them complete coverage from the entry. To her left, Maryse hurried down the ladder that led to the loft above the office. When she got about three feet from the ground, she pushed off the ladder and landed a foot from Jadyn and Colt.

"All set," Maryse said.

"Uh-huh." Colt looked her up and down. "Show me the hardware."

Maryse frowned and pulled out her cell phone. "Phone and camera," she said, pointing at the loft. "That's it."

Colt shook his head. "Don't make me have Jadyn frisk you."

Maryse sighed and pulled her nine millimeter from her jeans. "I only brought it to back you guys up. You should appreciate that."

Colt raised one eyebrow. "I saw Frank hauling your china cabinet into his woodshop this afternoon. Let's make a deal—I won't ask you about the bullet holes in it, and you get your gun back when you leave."

Maryse handed him the gun. "I hope you know what you're doing."

"I know exactly what I'm doing. I'm ensuring that you stay in that loft where you belong. I'm agreeing to this plan against my better judgment because I'm afraid you'd insinuate yourself into the situation anyway. By allowing you to participate, I maintain at least the illusion of control."

Jadyn laughed. Colt definitely had her cousin pegged.

He tucked Maryse's pistol in his waistband. "Okay. Tell me what you're going to do."

"I'm going to watch the back entrance," Maryse said, "and wait for Pickett to enter. Then I turn on the camera."

"Good. What else?"

"I don't move the camera at any time."

"And?"

She rolled her eyes. "I don't move from my position."

"Even if?"

"Even if everyone starts firing weapons."

"And?"

She threw her hands in the air. "Even if a parade of pygmy elephants tromps through the back wall. Even if QVC starts a half-off sale. Even if Daniel Craig shows up."

His lips quivered. "Well, maybe if pygmy elephants appear."

"I'm giving away my position if Daniel Craig shows up," Jadyn said.

Colt looked over at her.

"Just saying," Jadyn said.

Colt shook his head. "Pygmy elephants and Daniel Craig aside, is everyone ready? Because we've got about ten minutes until sunset. I figure Pickett will wait until dark to make his move."

"Ready," Maryse said.

Jadyn nodded.

"I'm ready to get this over with!" Helena yelled from the loft. "I'm hungry."

Jadyn glanced upward and saw Helena standing at the railing of the loft. She was completely decked out in camo, down to the paint on her face, except for the pink pumps that had likely gone out of style before Jadyn was even born. Maryse had said it was a "throwback" problem and she'd explain later. Helena had been so pissed off about it, she'd stomped through the hotel so hard Jadyn wondered if she could break an ankle.

Even if you removed the outfit from the equation, Jadyn was quite happy that she'd be floor level with potential gunfire if the only other option was in the loft listening to Helena. Maryse would need a strong drink when this was over. Maybe even therapy.

"Okay," Colt said, "then let's all get in our places. Remember to put your phone on silent and cover it where the screen light won't give you away. If anyone sees or hears anything, text the others and give a location for the activity."

"He's going down," Maryse said and gave them both a high five before scrambling up the ladder to the loft.

Jadyn moved to her position behind a pile of tires about fifteen feet behind Pickett's Cadillac while Colt took his spot behind a stack of crates near the front of the Cadillac. Nothing else left to do, she sat on a set of tires and prepared to wait.

She didn't have to wait long.

Only twenty minutes after they'd taken their places, a loud creak signaled the opening of the back door. They'd tested it earlier and Jadyn had no doubt the sound came from that entry point.

A minute later, Pickett emerged from the dark corner near the back door and walked into the dimly lit center of the shop. He looked around, then when he spotted his car, made a beeline for the far end of the shop where the Cadillac was still on the hydraulic lift that Colt had used earlier.

Pickett located the lift lever on the wall and raised the car, then pulled out a screwdriver and immediately went to work on the gas tank. It didn't take him much time to get the box removed from the tank, but then Jadyn figured he'd probably been using that device for some time.

He made quick work of the box and pulled out the black bag. In the quiet of the shop, Jadyn could hear the marbles they'd put in the bag clinking together, but the charade would only hold another second. Pickett felt the bag and frowned, then loosened the string and poured the marbles into his hand. He cursed and flung them across the shop, the pings echoing across the open building.

That was all they needed.

Colt stepped out from behind the crates, his gun leveled at Pickett. "Don't move or I'll shoot."

Pickett whirled around to face Colt. His arm dropped to his side and the bag fell to the floor, scattering the remaining marbles across the shop.

"Sheriff Bertrand," Pickett said, trying to pull an innocent look and failing completely. "I just wanted to check on my car. I couldn't make it here during regular business hours but the back door was open. I know it's trespassing, but I didn't think the owner would mind."

"That's a nice story," Colt said. "We'll see if a jury believes it, especially after they see the pouch of diamonds I have tucked away."

Pickett sneered, dropping all pretense of innocence. "I've gotten out of far worse than this. Do you really think someone like me works without a backup plan?"

"Then it's your backup plan against mine," Colt said. "Now,

turn around, get down on your knees, and put your hands on your head."

Pickett turned around, then launched for a toolbox about five feet away, pulling a pistol from his waistband as he went. Jadyn moved to the far side of the tires, trying to see if she had a shot, but her line of sight was blocked by a stack of cardboard boxes.

Pickett began firing and Colt dove for cover behind a car frame that offered minimal coverage.

"They're shooting!" Helena screamed from the loft and Jadyn looked up to see the ghost scrambling down the ladder as fast as the pumps allowed. A couple seconds later, there was an enormous crash and she looked over to see Helena emerge from a pile of hubcaps.

Jadyn checked Colt's position and her chest tightened so hard it hurt. If Pickett could manage a shot, even inches to the right, he'd have a bull's-eye. She gripped her pistol, preparing to fire through the cardboard boxes and hope for a hit, when Colt returned fire from the far end of the car body.

Pickett screamed and she knew he'd been hit, but had no way of knowing if the hit had incapacitated him. She crept around the edge of the tires as Colt inched across the shop toward the toolbox. He whipped around the back and Jadyn heard Pickett cry out again. A couple seconds later, Colt dragged him from behind the toolbox and pulled handcuffs from his pocket.

Jadyn let out a sigh of relief and she watched Colt click the handcuffs in place.

"So nice of you to do our dirty work," a man's voice sounded from the rear of the shop. "The man turned out to be such a liability to the organization."

Jadyn ducked down and peered between the tires. The voice sounded familiar...too familiar.

Oh my God! Agent Ross.

CHAPTER SIXTEEN

JADYN SUCKED IN A BREATH. Suddenly, it all made sense. The second crew had kidnapped Raissa because they knew the family had someone in the FBI on payroll but didn't know who. When they found Raissa and Zach, two FBI agents, in a car just like Pickett's, they must have assumed Raissa and Zach had confiscated Pickett's car and planned on keeping the merchandise for themselves.

Ross's sudden attitude shift toward Colt had nothing to do with his investigation and everything to do with their finding the Cadillac in the pond. Ross was looking for Pickett's stolen Cadillac and was afraid Colt and Jadyn had stumbled across it before he could locate it. His insistence that he inspect the car before the forensics team arrived now made perfect sense.

She watched as Ross walked into the light, his gun trained on Colt.

"Put down your weapon," Ross said, "and kick it over to me."

Jadyn could see Colt gauging his options, but there was nowhere he could hide before Ross emptied a magazine into him. Colt leaned over and placed his pistol on the ground, then kicked it over to Ross.

"Why am I not surprised you're dirty?" Colt asked.

Ross smirked. "You think the federal government is without complicity? Half of the things they do under the guise of protecting the public only serves their own interests and lines the pockets of executives. The rest of us risk our lives only to give them more power over us and make them wealthy."

"That's what you tell yourself," Colt said.

"I don't have to tell myself anything. My bank account speaks for itself."

"How did you know the cars were here?" Colt asked.

"When I was looking for that thief Bart, I saw Pickett parking a rental car on one of the back streets. I figured there was only one reason he'd be in Mudbug, so I had him followed."

"And he led you straight here."

Ross waved his pistol toward the loft. "Who's up there?"

"No one."

"I heard a crash when we came through the window." He looked to his left. "Check it out."

Stepford emerged from the shadows and headed across the shop toward the loft.

Maryse!

Jadyn watched as Stepford approached the area, praying that Helena made a noise somewhere else, distracting him from the loft. Then she caught sight of Helena, standing next to a stack of boxes. She swung at them like a prizefighter, but with each pass, her hands went right through them.

"I can't touch them," Helena wailed and swung so hard, she spun herself around and fell to the ground.

Stepford walked up to the ladder and looked up. "Come down or I start shooting through the roof."

Maryse rose slowly from the loft floor, her hands in the air, and carefully made her way down the ladder.

"You?" Stepford looked surprised. "It's LeJeune's wife," he yelled and pushed Maryse toward Ross.

Ross cursed. "Like I need the shitstorm her murder is going to bring." He glared at Maryse. "Why can't you stay at home and bake cookies like a good little wife?"

"Why don't you kiss my ass?" Maryse shot back.

Panic flooded Jadyn. While she appreciated her cousin's backbone, she had no doubt Ross intended to kill Maryse. Jadyn pulled her cell phone from her pocket and texted Mildred.

Ross and Stepford dirty. Maryse and Colt captive. Get backup.

She knew the hotel owner was in her office, cell phone in one hand and the other poised over her landline. Jadyn had no doubt that Mildred would raise a cavalry worthy of a small war.

But would they make it in time?

"Where's your girlfriend, the game warden?" Ross asked.

"Arresting the guy who was chopping cars," Colt said.

Jadyn watched Ross closely, trying to see if he bought Colt's lie. He studied Colt for several seconds, but Colt must be a convincing liar because Ross finally broke his stare and looked over at Stepford.

"What do you want to do with them?" Stepford asked.

"Later. First, I want the diamonds." Ross looked at Colt. "Where are they?"

"In my safe-deposit box," Colt replied.

"Mudbug doesn't have a bank with safe-deposit boxes, but have it your way. When you're dead, we'll search your house. If I don't find the diamonds there, I'll kill everyone in the sheriff's department and search there. The one thing I won't do is leave this town without the boss's product."

Jadyn's pulse pounded so hard she thought her head and chest would burst. She had no doubt Ross would live up to everything he said. He couldn't afford for any of them to be left alive or his entire life unraveled. But with Stepford holding Maryse and Colt with nowhere to hide, could she risk firing? She was good, but she imagined Ross and Stepford were no slouches. Her odds of taking out both of them before one of them took out Maryse or Colt were slim to none.

She looked across the garage, silently willing Helena to stop stressing and make something happen. The instant the thought crossed her mind, the ghost stopped her whirlwind arm routine and looked her direction. Jadyn waved toward Maryse and Colt, hoping Helena would understand that she wanted her to abandon what wasn't working and figure out some form of disruption now. A couple seconds later, Helena set off at a dead run. Jadyn prayed she had a plan but didn't have much hope.

"I say we just kill them and get out of here," Stepford said. "Every minute we're in this town we risk exposure."

"What about me?" Pickett said. "I'm not going to tell who you are—hell, I don't even know who you are. What say you cut me loose and let me get back to work for the families?"

"No can do," Ross said. "You've seen me and that makes you a threat. I don't leave loose ends."

Jadyn watched, helpless, as Ross leveled his gun at Pickett. Could she risk a shot now that Ross's weapon wasn't trained on Colt? She gripped her pistol and took aim through the tires, but no matter how she maneuvered the weapon, she didn't have a clear shot at Ross. Too much of him was protected by the toolbox.

And then Helena struck.

The ghost managed to run—sorta—about halfway across the shop when her ankles and the pumps had a massive disagreement about gravity. Down she went in a fall so hard, Jadyn could practically feel it in her own bones. But the fall didn't stop there. On her way down, she tipped over a box of parts and they spilled out, clanking in succession on the concrete floor. For her final parting shot, her right leg got tangled in power strip and she turned it on, activating a huge shop fan.

Things couldn't have taken more than a couple of seconds, but to Jadyn, everything played in slow motion. Stepford set off in the direction of the noise. At the same time, Ross fired a shot at Pickett, who rolled to the side, narrowly missing being shot. Maryse ran for the back door as Colt sprang for a crowbar on the other side of the toolbox from Ross.

But he wasn't going to make it.

Jadyn saw Ross's pistol leveled at Colt, and she rushed around the side of the tires, but still didn't have a clear shot. Desperate for anything to stop him from firing, she scanned the area surrounding Ross and zeroed in on a lift button on the wall. Without hesitating, she fired at the button.

The chain holding a car engine above Ross let go and the engine plummeted down, directly on top of Ross. Stepford turned around and spotted her, then started running in her direction. But the giant shop fan was his undoing. The wind current pushed the marbles from the gem bag across the floor in front of him. He took one step on the rolling glass, then another, and his legs flew out from under him.

He hit the ground as hard as Helena, but Stepford didn't get up. He didn't even move.

Jadyn ran around the tires and over to Stepford to relieve him of his pistol. Pickett still rolled around on the ground, screaming that he was shot. Colt gave him a glance before running behind the toolbox to check on Ross. When he walked back around, he looked at Jadyn and shook his head. She felt a bit of disappointment that Agent Ross wouldn't answer for his crimes, but dead was just as effective. Stepford could answer for all their ills.

Sirens sounded close by as Maryse ran into the middle of the shop, sliding to a stop next to Pickett. "Is he all right?" she asked.

"The shot nicked him," Colt said. "He'll live."

Maryse trotted up to Stepford and picked up his head then let it drop back down, his jaw smacking into the concrete. "Ooops. He slipped."

"Uh-huh." Jadyn grinned at Maryse.

"Sure," Helena bitched. "Worry about everyone else while I'm tied up like a rodeo calf."

Maryse coughed, covering her grin with her hand. Seconds later, the state police along with Colt's deputies dashed in the back door.

As Colt doled out explanations and instructions, Maryse made her way over to Helena to untangle her from the cord. The last Jadyn saw of the ghost, she gave the cord the finger then stomped through the wall of the shop, probably headed straight to the hotel for cobbler and a hot shower.

"I'm innocent!" Pickett yelled as two paramedics lifted him from the floor. "I'm just a civilian caught in the middle. They have no proof."

"We have video," Maryse said.

Pickett whirled around to stare at her, his jaw dropped.

"Video of you going straight for the box on the gas tank and opening the bag inside," Maryse said. "No jury in the world will believe it was an accident. I suggest you enjoy the last bit of freedom you're ever going to have…in the hospital."

Pickett's shoulders slumped and he allowed the paramedics to lead him away. Two stunned FBI agents trailed behind. A couple of paramedics lifted a groggy Stepford onto a stretcher and hauled him out, along with the last two agents in Ross's crew. They both looked shell-shocked, and Colt didn't relish the questioning the agents would receive back at the bureau. Someone would have to answer for Ross's ascension and their failure to notice that one of their own had been compromised.

Colt's deputies stared down at Ross, shaking their heads.

"I can't believe he was dirty," Deputy Nelson said. "Did the engine just fall on him?"

Colt started to speak and Jadyn interrupted. "Yeah. It was weird, but really good timing."

"I'll say," Deputy Nelson said. "Somebody should tell Marty to get that lift checked before it kills someone that matters."

"I'll be sure and do it," Colt said.

Deputy Nelson gave them a nod and headed after the paramedics, carefully avoiding another look at Ross. He'd turned slightly green at the first one.

Colt turned to her. "Why didn't you tell them you made that shot?"

"I don't want the attention it would bring, especially from the FBI. If we don't give them any reason to ask more questions, they're probably going to retreat to their corporate headquarters and try to figure out how to spin the Ross problem."

"True. I have to tell Marty something about his lift. The sheriff's department will pay, of course, but he'll want to know what happened."

"Then tell him there was so much cross fire, we're not sure," Jadyn said. "I know sometimes it doesn't seem like it, but I'm trying to have a relatively quiet existence in Mudbug."

Colt smiled. "And this is the sort of thing small-town legends are made of."

"Something like that."

He leaned over and whispered, "Well, it was damned impressive."

Jadyn smiled. "Yeah, it kinda was."

CHAPTER SEVENTEEN

AT 10:00 A.M., Colt knocked on Bart's front door, Jadyn standing beside him. It had been a long night of questioning with the FBI and the state police, but finally, everyone had seemed satisfied that they had the facts and a little more than depressed with the complicity of two FBI agents.

After all the activity, Colt thought he'd have no trouble falling asleep, but instead he'd lain in bed awake for at least another hour. His mind whirled with everything that had happened—Raissa's kidnapping, the diamonds, the showdown in the garage, and the incredible shot that Jadyn made. The shot that quite literally saved his life.

Everything from start to finish had gone down so quickly that he hadn't had time to process it all, much less dwell on the meanings and implications of everything that had happened. But in the quiet of his bedroom, it all came crashing back in a jumble, begging him to put it all into perspective.

The crime had been easy. He had plenty of experience processing criminal activity, even crimes that included dirty cops. Everything that had happened with Jadyn, however, was a whole different story, and one he hadn't managed to classify before finally falling asleep near dawn.

"His truck's here," Jadyn said, after a minute of waiting with no answer.

Colt knocked again.

A couple seconds later, the sound of a power tool echoed from the shop.

"He must be working," Colt said as he left the porch and headed for the shop. With every step, he imagined how this would go down. He hoped Bart wouldn't cause any trouble, but if life had taught him one thing, it was that you never really knew someone.

Out of courtesy, he banged on the metal door. He hadn't bothered with a warrant, but with Jadyn along, he didn't need one. Her jurisdiction extended to Bart's shop given that they had probable cause to believe this is where the crime originated. He waited several seconds, then banged again, figuring Bart might not be able to hear him over the tool noise.

A couple seconds later, the tool shut off and then Bart swung the door open. He looked tired and worried and when he focused in on them, both grew worse.

"Can we come in?" Colt asked.

He stepped back and they walked inside. In the center of the shop was a platform with some wheels on it. A large object just to the right was covered with a tarp. Colt frowned. He had hoped for cooperation, but he hadn't expected Bart to invite them in to see him in the process of committing a crime.

Bart grabbed a rag and wiped his hands. "I hope you two aren't here to grill me about my camp. I got detained yesterday by the New Orleans police because of that asshole from the FBI. I was ready to kill him." He gave them a sheepish look. "I probably shouldn't say that to the two of you."

"Nobody likes Agent Ross," Colt said.

Everything that had gone down the night before was all still very hush-hush. The FBI was in a panic, trying to figure out how they'd allowed a dirty agent to reach Ross's position in the agency without anyone catching on, and their attorneys and public relations people were racing in damage control mode. The secret wouldn't keep forever, but Colt had no problem keeping his mouth shut. The last thing he wanted to do was relive last night over and over again for every resident in Mudbug. The ole "I'm not allowed to talk about a federal investigation" excuse was the perfect out.

"We're not here about the camp," Colt said. "We're here about the cars."

Bart's expression immediately shifted to fear. "What cars?"

"The cars you've been stealing and chopping. We've already seen the car parts, and we found what's left of stolen cars dumped in one of the channels just west of here."

Bart looked back and forth between them, his hesitation clear. Finally he sighed. "It wasn't me."

Colt frowned. "Don't make it harder on any of us by lying."

"I'm not lying." He walked to a desk sitting on the front wall and pulled a plastic container out of the bottom drawer. "I have receipts for every part in this shop."

Colt looked at Jadyn, whose eyes widened. She gave him a slight shake of her head, indicating she was just as confused as he was.

"I don't understand," Colt said. "Why would you buy used car parts when you don't work on cars?"

Bart shuffled his feet, looking down at the concrete floor, then finally sighed. "I'll show you, but if it's possible, I don't want anyone to know."

"Ok," Colt said. "If it's possible."

Bart started across the shop and waved them over to the tarp-covered object. He flipped the tarp over the edges of the object until he could pull the entire piece of plastic off to one side. Colt stared at the jumble of metal, completely confused.

Jadyn's jaw dropped and she took one step forward, then ran her finger around a wheel. "It's industrial art."

Colt narrowed his eyes at the pile as Jadyn took a step back.

"It's a skyline," she said.

"Yeah," Bart said, looking pleased. "It will be the Detroit skyline when I'm done."

Colt stepped back next to Jadyn and looked at the mass of parts again, this time trying to view the entire thing rather than the individual pieces. He blinked a couple of times, then when his eyes cleared, the full effect of the piece came into focus.

"I see it now," he said. "You mean to tell me you've been hiding artwork in here?"

"Yeah," Bart said, a blush creeping up his neck. "I mean, Mudbug isn't exactly the kind of place that a man wants to run around saying he's an artist. Not if he plans on being treated like a man for very long."

Colt nodded. It was unfortunate but probably true. Mudbug wasn't exactly the artistic mecca of the South. "So do you sell these in art shops or something?"

"I did at first, but word got around and some people really liked the work, so now I mostly do commissioned pieces."

Jadyn smiled. "That's great. Where is this one going? Or can you say?"

"An automobile museum in Detroit," Bart said. "This is my biggest commission so far. It's kinda got me stressed."

Jadyn nodded. "So the real reason you only work three days a week is because you're doing this instead of construction."

"Yeah, pretty much."

"This is great," Colt said, "and I don't doubt it's on the up and up, but someone in Mudbug *is* chopping cars." He narrowed his eyes at Bart. "You didn't seem surprised when I told you why I was here, which means you already knew about it. And I'm guessing you know who's responsible."

Bart's face fell and he nodded. "I've had a bad feeling for some time that things were wrong, but I never imagined something criminal. After you left the other day, I decided to confront him and get a straight answer."

"It's Tyler, isn't it?" Jadyn asked.

Bart looked a little surprised at her guess, but nodded. "Yeah. I didn't want to believe it, but I walked right in on him in his barn while he was taking the hood off a car. There were several others, all stripped down. It didn't take a genius to know what was going on."

"What happened?" Colt asked.

"I told him it was only a matter of time before you found out and he had to stop. He lost it. Started screaming and yelling nonsense, saying it was all my fault because I didn't promote him back when we were working construction in New Orleans. That he couldn't make a living shrimping and I was getting rich."

Bart's expression was pure misery. "I couldn't promote him in New Orleans. He wasn't ready and mistakes on commercial jobs can get people killed. I had no idea he'd been mad at me over it this whole time. Anyway, I didn't know what to do, so I just left. I had a piece to deliver. I thought maybe I'd figure out something while I was driving, but I couldn't think of any way to fix this."

Bart looked at Colt. "What's going to happen to him?"

"I'll arrest him," Colt said, "and he'll get his day in court. If you want to help, then see to it that he gets a good lawyer. You might also be allowed to speak on his behalf if this goes to trial."

Bart nodded. "Thanks."

Jadyn reached out and squeezed his arm. "I'm really sorry."

"Yeah. Me too."

Jadyn looked up at Colt and he motioned toward the door. They walked silently out of the shop, leaving Bart to his thoughts.

When he pulled away from Bart's place, Colt looked over at Jadyn, who sat quietly.

"How did you know it was Tyler?" he asked.

"It was something in his expression. He looked scared but also sad. I figured there was only one person he'd be sad over. But I still don't understand why Tyler would blame Bart for everything just because he wasn't ready for a promotion."

"I doubt that's the only reason. Tyler's spent his entire life playing second fiddle to Bart—football, grades, women, job—so I guess he decided to create something he could do successfully and alone."

"So this was Tyler's way of doing something to get himself ahead. Something that Bart couldn't best him at?"

"I'm sure that's part of it, but don't ever discount cold hard cash. Shrimpers aren't making what they used to. And Bart's three-day workweek had probably been eating away at Tyler for a long time."

She nodded. "So are we going to arrest Tyler now?"

"Yeah. Might as well get this over with."

———

JADYN WAS in Mildred's office, filling her and Helena in on Tyler's arrest when Maryse burst into the office, panting.

Mildred jumped out of her chair. "What's wrong?"

"Nothing," Maryse said. "Everything's right. Zach is awake!"

Maryse threw her arms around Mildred and twirled the hotel owner around in the tight space until the two were stumbling. Jadyn felt the last of the weight she'd been carrying dissolve away and smiled as Helena laughed and clapped. Finally, Maryse released the hotel owner and they stared at each other, huge smiles on their faces.

"Well, don't just stand there grinning like idiots," Helena said. "Give us the details."

"I don't know a lot," Maryse said, "but Raissa called to say that Zach was out of the coma and doesn't appear to have any damage. They'll run tests, of course, but oh my God, isn't that great news?"

"The best," Jadyn agreed.

"And when I think about how it all went down and how badly it could have turned out," Maryse said, "it's just a miracle."

Mildred nodded. "Definitely a miracle."

Maryse looked over at Helena. "And you—if you're going to be of any use, you're going to have to be more accurate."

Helena crossed her arms across her chest and slumped down in the chair. "How was I supposed to know the importance of Ross saying 'the' boss instead of 'my' boss? I thought he was talking to someone at the FBI, not some Mafia guy. You would have thought the same thing."

"Maybe," Maryse said, "but if I'd repeated those exact words to Jadyn or Colt, they might have clued in to what was really going on and we wouldn't have been ambushed. I know everything turned out all right...well, not for Ross, but who cares...but I'd like to avoid a repeat. So, accuracy is king."

"Yeah, yeah." Helena waved a hand in dismissal. "You've turned into such a nag."

Maryse rolled her eyes and looked at Jadyn. "What's up with Tyler?"

"Colt arrested him this morning. He didn't resist, which made it easier on all of us. Bart offered to pay for his attorney. I guess we'll see if Tyler smartens up enough to accept."

"What a stupid thing for him to do," Maryse said. "I know shrimping doesn't pay all that well lately, but there's other ways Tyler could have made some extra money."

Mildred sighed. "My guess is he wanted the easiest route to Bart's lifestyle. It's all a shame, really. If he'd bothered to talk to Bart, he probably would have been able to get back into construction. Even if he was never as good as Bart, Tyler would have made far more money welding than he did shrimping."

"Pride often leads to foolish decisions," Jadyn agreed. "Have you told Luc the details of last night yet?" Luc was out of town for another day, but Jadyn knew Maryse planned on telling her husband what had happened before news of the events made it through the law enforcement community.

"I called him when I got home last night," Maryse said. "There was a lot of cussing and quite a few exclamations of disbelief, but overall, I got off easy. I think he's just happy that it's over."

"And the other situation?" Jadyn asked.

Maryse frowned. "Still unresolved. I'm landlocked until further notice."

"I'm sure it will all work out soon," Mildred said, obviously trying to cheer Maryse up.

Helena perked up. "Since you can't go out and pick stinkweed, will you take me to New Orleans to see Hank?"

"I may as well," Maryse said. "Let me call and see what time is good for them. With Lila due next month, I'm sure she has doctor's appointments and all sorts of other preparations going on."

Helena nodded. "I can't wait to see my grandbaby! I bet he's going to be beautiful."

Jadyn smiled. Helena's enthusiasm for her unborn grandson was infectious and kinda sweet.

"Make sure we go when Hank's not working," Helena said. "I know he's been putting in a lot of hours."

"I'll get a hold of him today," Maryse said, "and call Mildred with a time. Well, I've got to go talk to Frank about my hutch. I'll check in later."

And with that, Maryse sped out of the hotel as quickly as she'd arrived. Jadyn couldn't help but envy her cousin's energy.

"I best get going, too," Jadyn said. "I want to check in with Colt and see if there's anything I can help him with."

"Be sure and let him know the good news about Zach," Mildred said.

"It will be the first thing out of my mouth."

Jadyn left the hotel and strolled down the sidewalk. It was a beautiful summer day. The sun seemed to shine brighter. The breeze seemed cooler. But Jadyn knew it was all because things were right again in Mudbug.

Shirley greeted her with a huge smile when she walked into the sheriff's office. Colt emerged from his office, and his scowl turned to a grin as she told them about Zach's recovery.

Shirley grabbed a tissue and dabbed her eyes. "That's such good news."

Colt nodded. "The best news we've had all day. Do you know when he can have visitors?"

"No, but I'll let you know as soon as Maryse finds out. I have a feeling he's going to be a very popular patient."

"I'm sure of it," Colt agreed. "If you have some time, I have an update on the Pickett situation."

"Absolutely," Jadyn said and followed him back to his office.

Colt shut the door behind them but instead of sitting in his office chair like he usually did, he leaned against the side of the desk right next to the chair she sat in. Jadyn tried not to read anything into the fact that he hadn't placed the large bit of furniture in between them. It was clear by his relaxed posture that Colt was in good spirits. It might be as simple as that.

"After he saw the video, Pickett sang like a bird," Colt said. "He gave up the other crew and the New Orleans police have already picked them up. They'll get mug shots to Raissa, and now Zach, and I anticipate the whole thing will wrap up very nicely."

"It's incredible, the way everything turned out. It's what I hoped for, but so much better than what I expected."

Colt nodded. "From the beginning, I was afraid of how badly this could end. All indications led in the opposite direction of a positive outcome. This has been the biggest and most pleasant surprise of my entire law enforcement career."

"Well, let's just hope nothing ever tops it. I don't think I have the nerve to handle it."

Colt smiled. "You've got the nerve to handle damn near anything. That shot you made was nothing short of amazing." He extended his hand. "I haven't thanked you properly for saving my life."

She placed her hand in his, expecting to shake, but instead he tugged and she rose out of the chair to stand only inches in front of him.

"Thank you for saving my life," he said, his voice low.

Her heart pounded in her chest as she looked at him. "You're welcome."

He lowered his lips to her in a feathery kiss, then wrapped his arms around her and pressed his lips harder against hers, increasing the intensity.

Jadyn leaned into him and ran her hands up his strong back.

She had no idea what the future held, but at the moment, it looked promising.

Find out what Helena is up to next in Chaos in Mudbug.

For more information on books by Jana DeLeon, visit her website janadeleon.com.

Made in the USA
Middletown, DE
17 January 2022

58907716R00136